TWO GIRLS, A CLOCK, AND A CROOKED HOUSE

TWO GIRLS, A CLOCK, AND A CROOKED HOUSE

BY MICHAEL POORE

with illustrations by LEIRE SALABERRIA

Random House 🏠 New York

Text copyright © 2019 by Michael Poore
Jacket art and interior illustrations copyright © 2019 by Leire Salaberria

Visit us on the Web! rhcbooks.com

Educators and librarians, for a variety of teaching tools, visit us at RHTeachersLibrarians.com

Library of Congress Cataloging-in-Publication Data
Name: Poore, Michael, author.
Title: Two girls, a clock, and a crooked house / Michael Poore.
Description: First edition. | New York: Random House, [2019] | Summary: After Amy is struck by lightning, she and her silent friend, Moo, are able to communicate telepathically, travel through time, and face a child-eating witch.
Identifiers: LCCN 2018038823 | ISBN 978-0-525-64416-3 (trade) | ISBN 978-0-525-64417-0 (lib. bdg.) | ISBN 978-0-525-64418-7 (ebook)
Subjects: | CYAC: Time travel—Fiction. | Telepathy—Fiction. | Friendship—Fiction. | Witches—Fiction.
Classification: LCC PZ7.1.P644 Two 2019 | DDC [Fic]—dc23

Printed in the United States of America
10 9 8 7 6 5 4 3 2 1
First Edition

Random House Children's Books supports the First Amendment and celebrates the right to read.

FOR JIANNA!

CONTENTS

TWO GIRLS, A CLOCK, AND A CROOKED HOUSE

1. THE CRIME EXPERIMENT

AMY WOOD WAS PLANNING to rob the Everything Store. You know the kind of store I mean. It's where you go to get prescriptions, and they also have dog food and Christmas lights and . . . well, everything. Anyhow, at Halloween time they sold these hoodies that looked like butterflies, and Amy planned to steal one.

One Friday afternoon, she hopped onto her bike after school and headed for the store.

It wasn't an impulse. No one had dared her to do it.

She didn't *need* a hoodie to keep warm. She didn't have a disease where she couldn't help stealing or didn't know any better.

It was an experiment. She simply wanted to see if she could do it without getting caught. She had an argument with herself as she rode down the street.

"I *think* I can get away with it," she said to herself (a parallel-dimension self, visible in her rearview mirror).

"On the other hand," Self said back, "there's a strong probability that you will be arrested and sent to prison."

"I have planned carefully," she reassured Self.

Amy *always* planned her experiments carefully. Even last summer's Ketchup Experiment—which had been a mess and a disaster—had been well planned. The ketchup wasn't supposed to end up on her mother. But you couldn't control everything, or it wouldn't be an experiment, right? Right.

She rolled across the Everything Store parking lot and parked her bike by the door.

Inside, she said "Hi" to the clerk in an offhand, un-interested, ten-year-old kind of way and slipped off down the cosmetics aisle.

"Rbblmmgh," mumbled the clerk, barely looking up.

Amy's heart beat fast. She couldn't decide whether she was thrilled or frightened. Was there a difference?

Focus! she told herself.

She glanced at the big round mirror up in the corner of the ceiling. The clerk, theoretically, could see down every aisle, from everywhere in the store. Fortunately, Amy had planned for this.

She would create a diversion.

The diversion was something she had prepared ahead of time: a plastic sandwich bag full of orange pop and crushed cereal. Now, at the store, she removed it from her pocket, pulled off the twist tie, and dumped the contents onto the floor between the sunglasses and the school supplies.

Then she poked her head around the endcap, waved at the clerk, and politely shouted, "Sir? I think someone threw up in aisle three. It's really repulsive."

The clerk—who looked like a stick with a beard—sighed and mumbled, "All right. Thanks, I guess."

Amy retreated into the painkiller/wound care aisle and waited until she heard the clerk get a mop and a bucket and head for the school supplies. Then she fast-walked halfway across the store to where the hoodies were kept stacked in a plastic tub.

She checked the big round mirror. It was hard to tell what she was looking at, the way everything seemed to bend and recede down a black hole, but it kind of looked like the clerk was bent over, facing away. Good.

Quickly Amy grabbed one of the hoodies and dove into it like you would a swimming pool (it was waaaaay too big), shooting her arms through the sleeves, popping her head out the top, and smoothing the whole thing until the bottom hem hung around her knees. Then she walked toward the door, between the shampoo and the greeting cards, just as casual as could be.

Time seemed to slow down. Second by second, she was sure that NOW was the moment the clerk would call out, "Wait a second there, kid!" NOW was the moment his hand would come down on her lawbreaking, butterfly-winged shoulder; NOW was the moment her dark prison journey would begin. . . .

The Crime Experiment was a mistake, she realized (too late).

And sure enough, here came the footsteps behind her.

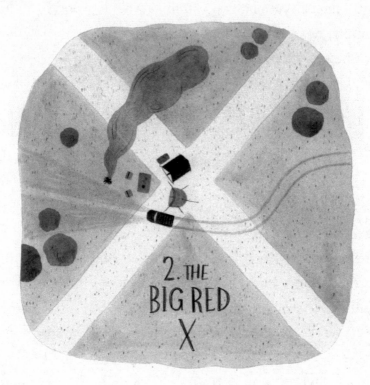

2. THE BIG RED X

AMY'S HEART WENT TURBO.

Should she run? Maybe she could just act like she'd tried the hoodie on and forgotten to take it off. Maybe—

Behind her, a closet door opened—like a supply closet, where the mop lived.

"Have a nice day," called the clerk.

"'Kay," said Amy, and just like that she was out the door and safe.

And on her bike, riding down the street with wings

fluttering behind her, two antennae wobbling and bending atop her head.

She was a magical creature. Booyah!

Her experiment was a success! Double booyah! Her conclusion? Diversion tactics were a highly effective way of getting away with stuff. Tomorrow she would bring the hoodie back. She wasn't interested in being a real criminal, after all.

Amy Wood, pseudo criminal and pseudo butterfly, headed for home.

Now, ordinarily it would have taken Amy about twenty seconds to get home. She and her parents lived just five doors down from the Everything Store.

The thing was, Amy wasn't riding in the direction of the house.

Why not?

Because she and her parents were not living at their house.

Where were they living?

You'll see.

Amy rode her bike completely out of the neighborhood, onto a road that led into the country.

About ten minutes later, she stopped beside an open field full of dirt.

In the middle of the dirt, someone had painted a giant red **X** on the ground.

In the middle of the X, a sort of camp had been set up. Some tents, a table, and an old Jeep. In the middle of the camp sat two people on folding chairs, sipping coffee.

These were Amy's mother and father, and this camp was where they had been living for the past two weeks.

"Hi!" Amy said to them, and they looked glad to see her and said, "Hello, Offspring!"

They didn't mention the hoodie.

Dad said, "School?"

Amy reported that school had been fine, if unremarkable.

"How was *your* day?" she asked.

"It got warmer for a while," said Mom. "We had lunch. Now it's getting a little colder."

This was the kind of report you could expect if your parents sat on camp chairs all day long in the middle of a field.

There was a reason they were living in tents, out in the middle of the dirt.

You could see the reason if you peered across the field. At the edge of the field were some trees, and beyond the trees was a machine as big as a five-story building. It had decks like a ship, and tangles of pipes, and smokestacks and cables and wheels and engines. The machine had one enormous metal arm, like the arm of a crane, and at the end of this arm was a great iron claw.

The machine was called the Big Duke.

The Big Duke was famous because it was the biggest mining machine in the whole world. It was visible from space, they said. Certainly, it was visible from the highway, where people had begun pulling over to take pictures. You could even see tiny people on it, running around with wrenches and things.

When the Big Duke reached the red X, according to the TV news, its claw would start tearing up the earth, digging up hyperzantiummetachondrite (a green substance used to make tennis balls). Scientists had discovered that there was a lot of hyperzantiummetachondrite in the ground all around Troy (the town where Amy and her parents lived).

So why were Amy's mom and dad camped out on the big red X?

Because they were scientists, just like Amy. They worked at a fancy university in the city and did experiments for a living.

That's how they knew that when the Big Duke started digging up hyperzantiummetachondrite, it was going to do all kinds of toxic things to the ground.

"The water in the ground will turn into something like poop," Mom and Dad had told the TV people. "Kids who live around here will start getting all kinds of horrible mutant diseases." But the TV people didn't put them on TV.

"They'll put it on TV when it's too late," Dad often

growled, "after people start growing extra heads and their livers come squirting out of their belly buttons."

Sometimes when Mom and Dad talked about the Big Duke, they got really mad and turned red in the face.

"I'm sick and tired of seeing big companies with tons of money make life worse for people!" Dad had shouted once. "And people just *let* them do it!"

"Not all people," Mom had reminded him. If nothing else, she said, there were the people here in this little camp, the Wood family. If nothing else, there were three people who understood how important it was to stand up and fight when something was hurting people, even if that something was as big as a mountain.

Two weeks ago, when the machine first loomed over the edge of town, Mom and Dad had decided to go live in the field. The Big Duke couldn't dig, they reasoned, if there were people sitting right on top of the target.

"A *protest* experiment," Mom had explained.

Sometimes people drove by and yelled jokes at her parents and called them names. Called them "hippies" and "freaks" and "eggheads" and "troublemakers."

Mom and Dad tried not to let this bother them.

"Don't let it bother *you*, either," they advised Amy.

It did *not* bother Amy, who thought having scientists for parents was just about the coolest thing in the world.

It made them interesting. It made life one great big experiment.

She parked her bike beside a folding camp table.

Dad said, "It's going to get pretty chilly tonight. Why don't you put a sweater on while I boil dinner?"

"Um," said Amy, "I sort of *am* wearing a sweater already, sort of."

She waggled her head to make the antennae bounce.

Dad blinked at her. "Ah," he said. "Well, good, good." Then he got up to go boil the water.

It would probably not occur to Dad to wonder where the butterfly hoodie had come from. Dad was not a detail person.

As usual, dinner conversation was about exciting things happening at the university.

"Professor Peel is writing a paper," Mom was saying. "He says there aren't just black holes; there are orange and purple holes, too."

"I heard about that," said Dad. "But I also heard that other labs have challenged his results. Just like Professor Ziz and his time particle."

"Oh yeah," said Mom. "The guy who says time is like boiling water."

Dad frowned. "What do you think he means by that?" he asked. "'Time is like boiling water'?"

Mom shrugged. "He hypothesizes that it moves. He

says you could move around in it, like a swimmer or a piece of potato, if you knew how."

Most nights Amy made an effort to contribute to the conversation. Not tonight, though.

Amy's father looked at her and asked, "Whatcha thinking?"

"Maybe she's not thinking anything," said her mother. "Maybe she has died, right there in her chair, and hasn't fallen over yet."

Amy's parents had learned that the best way to get her to open up was to talk about her like she wasn't there.

"I doubt it," replied her dad. "If she had died, she would start to smell."

Her mom gave the air a sniff.

"She *does* smell," said Mom. "Just the slightest. Well, that's sad, isn't it? We'll have to go online and order a new child."

"In the meantime," said Dad, "I may as well finish her freeze-dried macaroni."

Amy broke the silence, brandishing her fork, protecting her plate.

"Not in this life!" she protested. "And if you really have to know, I was wondering how come you didn't notice I'm dressed like a butterfly."

"Hmmm," said her father. "Ah, yes."

"Where'd that come from?" asked Mom.

Amy told them about the experiment, and they listened and chewed without interrupting.

"Diversion tactics," said Dad. "Smart."

Mom kicked him under the table. He grimaced and said *"Mrrzzl!"* through his teeth. That was his way of saying a bad word without causing a stir.

"We'll talk about this more later," he said.

This was one advantage of having scientist parents. The regular, practical world sometimes puzzled them, and they needed time to sort things out. So you could come home with a stolen hoodie or a bad report card, and even though they knew these things were not good things, they didn't always know right away what to do about them. Sometimes they didn't get around to doing anything at all.

"I wish you'd spend more time with the other kids," said Mom, toying with a silver ring on her right pinkie finger. It had once belonged to Marie Curie and had been a graduation present from Grandma. The ring was the only piece of jewelry her parents owned, and Mom always fidgeted with it when something worried her.

"I *do* spend time with other kids," said Amy, talking with a mouthful of instant peas. "At school, every day."

"I mean, outside of school."

"Like who?" asked Dad. "She's the only ten-year-old on Cornish Road. You have to go, like, ten blocks."

It was true. Amy and her parents lived on the very edge

of the neighborhood, and all the kids on the neighboring blocks were either little tiny kids or high school kids who just grunted if she tried to speak to them.

"I'm friends with Moo," she said quietly.

Her parents didn't say anything for a while.

Then her dad said, "I'm not really sure that counts." Which wasn't very nice of him. Sometimes parents can be that way.

"Can I go over there?" Amy asked. "After we eat?"

Mom and Dad thought things over in their slow, fuzzy-headed way.

"Be back before darkish," said Mom.

Amy got up to make her escape before they thought to talk about the hoodie some more.

"Darkish," Amy called back over her shoulder. "Got it."

"Watch out for the witch," said Dad.

"'Kay," said Amy.

Dad's voice didn't sound like he was kidding around.

And that's because he wasn't.

3. THE HAUNTED WOODS

AMY PAUSED, ON HER way across the field, to pick up a rock. A nice rock, with some shiny bits in it.

The hoodie had big pockets in the front, the way most hoodies do. She stashed the rock in the left pocket and gave it a pat. Amy liked picking up rocks that seemed unique or pretty or weird. She did it a lot. It made her feel scientific, in a geology kind of way.

Upon reaching the road, she zipped off at top speed, antennae jiggling and wings flapping.

She had a nervous feeling in her stomach, because going to Moo's house was another kind of experiment. An adventure, in a way.

In order to get there, see, you had to get past the woods.

The woods where the witch lived. The witch who ate kids.

Seriously.

I know what you're thinking. *Oh, that's what kids always say, anyplace around the world.* The woods are always haunted. It's how kids are, Amy knew. Ghosts and witches everywhere. But this was different. Here's why:

The kids didn't start the rumors about a witch. They heard it from their parents.

"You need to stay out of the woods," Mom and Dad had warned Amy when she grew old enough to leave home on her bike.

"I know," she had answered. "You could get lost or fall in a hole."

"True," said Dad. "But there's also the witch."

Weird. Usually grown-ups said that there were no such things as witches.

"There are no such things as witches," said Amy experimentally, using reverse psychology.

"That's true," said Dad. "Except when it isn't."

Amy knew he was serious, because he didn't sound distracted or fuzzy headed for once.

"When I was a kid," he said, "there really *was* an old woman who lived there, in an old shack, and she took some kids and ate them."

"It's not for sure that she *ate* them," said Mom.

"She *disappeared* with them," said Dad. "That's an actual fact, like the speed of light."

"How do you *know* they disappeared?" Amy asked.

Dad started to say something, but Mom quietly said, "We just know."

Which was not like her mother, and not very scientific, but Amy was old enough to sense when grown-ups didn't want to talk about a thing anymore.

Other parents told their kids about the witch, too. It was like an official town secret, except everyone knew. Sometimes they talked about it at school. Kids dared each other to go into the woods, but no one ever did.

And so (you will recall that we were discussing Amy's bike ride out to Moo's house) the part of the trip that took Amy alongside the woods was something she did not look forward to.

On this particular evening, though, Amy felt protected by the butterfly hoodie. It was such a *happy* piece of clothing! Still, when she approached the trees, she held her breath just like when she passed a cemetery . . . held it, held it . . . and just as her lungs caught fire, the trees thinned out and fell away behind her.

Safe. Again.

She looked in her rearview mirror, where Parallel-Dimension Self was shaking her head.

"One of these days," warned Self, "your luck is gonna run out."

4. Moo

THE WOODS GAVE WAY to a cow pasture, and across from the pasture sat Moo's house.

Like an old man, the house leaned forward a little, as if using the front porch as a cane.

Sitting on the front-porch steps, facing the road and the open pasture, was a small girl.

She had dark hair, cut short, and humongous brown eyes. Intelligent eyes, but with a faraway look, as if she might be dreaming. Like Amy, the girl wore a hoodie, and, like Amy's hoodie, it was made to look like an animal. It was a cow hoodie, with big black spots. The hood had cow ears that stuck out and two plastic eyes that peered over the girl's head.

This was Moo.

"Hey," said Amy.

Moo didn't say anything back.

Moo never said anything at all.

Amy leaned her bike against the porch and sat down beside her.

Moo gave no indication she even knew Amy was there.

Sometimes this silence was one of the main things Amy liked about Moo. Other times, naturally, she wished Moo would at least say "Hello" or that it was a nice day.

But no. She might have been asleep, if it hadn't been for one thing: every once in a while, she *did* say something.

There were cows in the pasture, and now and then one of them would say, "MOOooooOOOOoooo."

And Moo would say it back: "Mooooooo!"

This, obviously, was why Amy called her Moo. (Presumably, Moo had a regular human name, but Amy didn't know what it was.)

Amy didn't really know very much about her friend at all, in fact. There were a million things she would have *liked* to know but didn't.

Here is a list of ten things Amy had asked Moo in the two years they'd been friends:

1. "How come you wear that cow hoodie all the time?"

2. "Do you have some kind of huge, multicolored, explosive wart on your head, under the hood?"

3. "Can I see it?"

4. "Would you rather eat a big plate of poop just once, or have to eat the same thing, every meal, for the rest of your life?"

5. "What's your favorite season? Mine's summer. No, wait . . . spring! No . . . fall."

6. "Do you even know I'm here?"

7. "Aren't you glad sharks swim instead of fly?"

8. "Is something wrong with your mom?" (Moo's mom lived in the leaning house, too. She was almost as quiet as Moo.)

9. "How come you never talk?"

10. "Do you remember how we met?"

Amy thought that this last question, more than any other, might inspire Moo to think, and remember, and speak up. So far, nada.

Sometimes Amy played a little mind movie in her head where Moo turned to her and said, "Why, yes, Amy, I remember. One day a couple of years ago, my mom brought me to your school, and the teacher assigned you to be my Welcome Buddy, to help me find the lunchroom and learn the rules at recess. And you were very nice, even if you felt sort of freaked out when I never moved or said anything. You were SO smart. . . . You figured out that if you took me by the hand, I would follow you places. I would even carry my lunch tray and eat. But at the end of the day, my mom came back and talked with the teacher and the school nurse, and all three of them seemed pretty disappointed. They had been hoping that all the activity at school would be contagious and I'd start talking. The next day, Mom didn't bring me back. Or the next, or the next.

"A couple of weeks later, you went speeding by my house on your bike. Then you came speeding back, and stopped, and came up on the porch and talked to me. And that's how we met and started being friends."

It was a great mind movie, but it hadn't come true so far. Moo simply wasn't one of those friends that you sing songs with, or dare to do things, or have long secret talks with. She was the kind of friend you had to use your imagination with. Here is a list of ways Amy had found to spend time with Moo:

1. Help Moo stare out over the pasture and the road.

2. Help Moo moo back at the cows.

3. Perform a news show about whatever was going on in Amy World. School stuff. Her experiments. All about the Big Duke and how her parents were playing chicken with the mining company.

4. Read aloud.

5. Fall asleep sitting in the glider.

Today Amy had brought a book and planned to read aloud. First, though, she hopped down one step, facing Moo, to show off the stolen hoodie.

"Isn't this the happiest hoodie you've ever seen?" she said, twirling. "If I were to decide to keep it, I'd only wear it on days when I got elected president or on Saturdays or if there was a field trip or if you were to say something. I can't keep it, though. It's not really mine."

And she told Moo about the experiment, just as she had told her parents.

"Oh!" she said suddenly. "I almost forgot. I brought you something!" And she reached into her pocket and took out the nice rock from the field. Sometimes she kept the rocks she found, and sometimes she felt like giving them to Moo.

"Sparkly, huh?" she said, holding the rock up where Moo could see it. Then she darted down to the end of the porch and set it atop a small pile of other rocks, from other evenings.

Sitting down again beside her friend, Amy opened the book she had brought. It was more of a notebook, actually. It was, in fact, a book of her own poems and drawings.

The first poem she read aloud was about the seasons. It went like this:

"What if everything changed color
in fall, instead of just leaves?
What if your house turned yellow like a big maple
leaf and came swishing down through the air and
landed in a pile of other houses?
What if all the books in the school turned red (like
BLOOD!!!!)
and a huge gust of wind came along and blew them
away like a cloud (of BLOOD!!!!)???
And what if I turned yellow and red mixed together
and flew away, too,
and never ever ever came down?"

Moo seemed to appreciate the poem. Don't ask me how Amy knew this. It was something Amy thought she could sense now and then.

"Wanna go see the cows?" Amy asked.

And Moo said, "Moo." Amy made an assumption that this stood for yes.

If you took Moo's hand and gave it a gentle tug, Amy

had learned through experiment, she would get up and follow you across the street and stand by the fence with you.

You had to get Moo's mom's permission for that, naturally.

Amy skipped up onto the porch and knocked at the screen door.

Knock, knock, knock!

Something shadowy and sad appeared on the other side of the screen.

"Hi, Moo's mom," said Amy.

"Hi," said Moo's mom, sounding tired. Through the screen, she always sort of looked and sounded like a candle that had gone out.

"Can I take Moo across the street to look at the cows?" Amy asked.

"Okay," said Moo's mom. "Watch the traffic."

Amy said, "We will," skipped back down, and took Moo by the hand. Moo rose to her feet like a mechanical toy set in motion and followed Amy across the yard.

Across the street, to the old wooden fence that formed the border between the People World and the Cow World. A couple of cows, some ways off, raised their heads thoughtfully and began wandering in the girls' direction.

The cows weren't marked in any way, and they didn't wear cowbells. They didn't belong to anyone, according to Amy's parents.

"They're wild cows," Mom had declared.

"Cows can be wild?" Amy had asked.

"A big ol' cow truck crashed," Dad had explained, "back when your mom and I were teenagers. These cows are the descendants of the cows from the crash. Their grandcows and great-grandcows."

"MooOOoo," said one of the cows, approaching close enough to have her nose rubbed.

"Moo," answered Moo.

Amy caressed the cow's nose (so soft—like a cupcake!). Moo raised her hand and copied.

A breeze kicked up, and Moo swayed with it, just a little. Sometimes her head moved as if she were listening to something only she could hear, looking at something only she could see.

After a while, Amy took Moo's hand again and led her friend back to the house. She retrieved her bike, told Moo, "Bye! See you when I see you!" and raced homeward.

She almost made it, too.

IT WASN'T THE WITCH that got Amy. Just the weather.

It grew windy in a big hurry as she was passing through the woods, and that wasn't a problem. Amy loved storms; she left her hood down so her hair would wave like a flag.

"It's like flying," remarked Self in the rearview mirror.

But the wind got even stronger. Amy's wings made buzzing, snapping noises, and the bike wobbled. Rain peppered her cheeks and the backs of her hands. Suddenly it seemed like a long way to the red X. She pedaled harder. Almost out of the woods now.

"It's a time experiment," she told Self, gritting her teeth and squinting. "Can the young scientist reach home in less time than it takes the storm to really, really get nasty?"

POW! She hit a dip in the pavement, wobbled, and almost crashed. Amy put her feet down and brought herself to a stop.

Staying dry wasn't worth a broken neck, she thought.

The sky had gotten darker in a way Amy didn't like. She pulled her hood up and yanked the drawstrings tight.

Suddenly she felt tingly all over. Felt all funny and electrical and bad. Her hair tried to stand up; it swelled inside her hood and came frizzing out around her face.

The witch! Oh my God!

Except it wasn't a witch, and she knew it. Any scientist would know.

She was about to get struck by lightning.

"*Mrrzzl,*" she said.

And then everything went very BRIGHT and it was like being stomped on by the sun.

5. EVERYTHING IS FUZZY

EVERYTHING WAS FUZZY.

First, there was some feeling in Amy's fingertips, and they felt like fuzzballs. As if her nerves were vibrating. Then there was some light, and that was fuzzy, too.

"Amy?"

Her mom's voice.

"Everything's fuzzy," Amy tried to say, but it came out "Obevizzzzizzizee" because her tongue and brain were fuzzy, too.

"What was that, sweetie? Try again."

Amy felt Mom take her hand. Felt someone else take her other hand. Dad?

"Maybe the speech part of her brain has been scrambled," Dad said.

"No big deal," Mom replied. "She can learn how to talk by tapping on things."

"I can hear you," Amy managed to say. "You guys suck."

She tried to get her eyes to focus. Her brain filled with warm, bright fuzz. Her ears and nose picked up what might be the noises and smells of a hospital.

"What happened?" she asked.

They patted her hands (fuzzily), and Dad said, "Lightning."

Wow! Seriously? A sudden panic grabbed her and squeezed.

"Oh God," she said, sitting upright. "Am I melted? Am I paralyzed?" She poked herself all over the place. "Did I partially explode? Is my brain exposed?"

"Yes," said Dad.

Amy heard Mom hit Dad and say, "ZACH-ary!"

"No," said Dad. "You're fine. They say your butterfly costume thing might have shielded you. The antennae conducted most of the voltage away from your head and shot it into the ground. Lightning is mysterious stuff."

"Is it burned up?" Amy asked.

"Baked," said Mom, "ever so slightly, on top. Surprisingly okay otherwise. It's in the little closet in the corner. You can wear it home if you want."

"So I'm fine?" she said. "Really, totally fine?"

And they answered her, told her yes, she was fine, but Amy tuned her parents out just then. She wasn't being rude. She was just distracted (and disturbed) by something.

Little glowing lights floated in the air over her parents' heads. Little lights in the shape of hearts.

Interesting. But Amy had a feeling it was not something she should mention to her parents, or doctors. Not if she wanted to go home, which she did.

"I'm going back to sleep for a while," she said, and lay down and closed her eyes.

"A fine and worthy idea," said Dad, blowing her a kiss.

Sleep rolled in like a high tide, carrying strange and curious dreams.

THE DOCTORS KEPT AMY in the hospital another day, testing her coordination, testing heart and organ function. Then they let Mom take her home.

They went back to their actual home, their actual house, instead of the camp.

"It's not necessary!" Amy protested. "I'm fine. I got As on all the tests."

"I want you to get one more really good night's rest," said Mom, "before taking on the world again. My decision is firm and unchangeable, like the gravitational constant of the universe."

"But Dad—"

"Dad will be just fine by himself for one night, probably. Now hush."

It turned out to be a wonderful idea. Amy hadn't realized how much she missed her real bed, and a real bathroom, and carpeting. There was more dust than usual, which was saying something; her parents were indifferent housekeepers. And there was a partly empty feeling, since Dad wasn't there. But other than that, it was nice and familiar and warm and . . . home.

Mom went out and brought back Mexican food, and they had a contest to see which of them could use the spiciest of the sauce packets without making a face. (Amy won.)

One thing, though, kept it from being a 100 percent comfort-fest.

The heart over her mom's head was still there, pulsing and pink. Amy liked this little vision, but it bothered her, too. That was the kind of thing people saw when their brains were mixed up, right? Except she didn't feel mixed up. She felt pretty sharp, actually, almost as if she'd been turned up a notch or two.

It wasn't just the heart, though. There were other oddities.

The accumulated dust, for example. It seemed to be accompanied by little dust ghosts that puffed and coughed along the shelves and sat sneezing on the furniture.

And the food! Something like a fire symbol blazed in the air over the red sauce.

Maybe if she slept well, in her own bed, her brain or her imagination would calm down.

It didn't help that her toothbrush appeared to be dripping with minty little icicles.

"It's not imaginary," said Parallel-Dimension Self in the bathroom mirror. "I'm imaginary; this other stuff is real. Deal with it."

Amy ignored her and went straight to bed (which was surrounded by warm, snoozy, half-visible clouds). She fell asleep with some difficulty, feeling a bit sorry for poor old Dad, alone out there in the field in his little tent. But her bed was soft and cloudy and familiar, and she *did* fall asleep at last.

She dreamed, for some reason, about frogs.

IN THE MORNING, AMY wanted to go to school.

Mom wasn't wild about the idea.

"It's been three days since the lightning," Amy argued. "Can I just go, and if I don't feel right, they can call you? I'm sure they know what happened, right, the school nurse and everything?"

Mom liked arguments that made sense. So she thought about it while they ate their eggs, and finally said yes. They even drove out to the camp so Amy could tell Dad hello and pick up her bike.

"Greetings!" said Dad, who was trying to make coffee over the fire. As Amy kissed him, the kettle boiled over. It always boiled over. Dad said, "Mrrzzl." Then he said, "School, eh?"

Amy said, "Yep."

"Well, good, I guess. They'll call us, I suppose, if you start to explode or catch fire."

Mom kicked him, then kissed him, and they waved goodbye as Amy headed for school.

6. THEY HAD YOUR SCHOOL PICTURE ON THE INTERNET

A T SCHOOL AMY WAS a star.

Her picture had been online and in the newspaper, because it wasn't often someone got hit by lightning, let alone a kid.

"They had your school picture on the internet," said a boy named Thomas. "It was the picture from last year, where your teeth looked gross."

When everyone was in their seats, Mrs. Barch, the teacher, said, "So you got struck by lightning." (Mrs. Barch was a thousand years old. She was going to retire at the end of the year.)

"Yes," said Amy.

"Did it hurt? You missed a reading quiz."

"It DID hurt," said Amy. "It was like . . . imagine if a bunch of hot needles went through you, going a hundred miles an hour."

Mrs. Barch had a way of staring when she talked to you. She had big, watery, ancient eyes that NEVER, EVER blinked. There was a school legend that Mrs. Barch had once hypnotized a kid and planted a command in his head that when he reached sixth grade, he would come to school in a dress, and he had done it.

Mrs. Barch was staring at Amy now while they talked.

Amy didn't feel hypnotized. She was, in fact, making an effort not to see certain things. Like, Mrs. Barch had a heart over her head, but it looked fossilized and had a Band-Aid on it.

Some of the kids in the class had little fires inside them. Others were surrounded by clouds of spirit-bubbles. All the kids had hearts over their heads. A couple of the hearts had Band-Aids like Mrs. Barch's.

"So," said Mrs. Barch, "are you traumatized?"

"Nope," said Amy. "I can deal."

"Well, that's fine," said Mrs. Barch. "Let's move on with

our lives, then, shall we? Open your social studies books to page fifty-three. Claudette, would you mind reading?"

A girl named Claudette started reading about a girl in Peru who raised llamas, and Amy's stardom came to an end.

She got over it. She moved on. She learned that llamas would spit in your face if you disrespected them.

AT THE RED X camp that night, Amy and her parents had a special treat: real macaroni and cheese for dinner. Mom made the best macaroni and cheese in the history of life. It came to the table in a big casserole dish and had a skin of baked cheese on top. Little cheese volcanoes bubbled and oozed. Then you'd stick a spoon in it and dump some onto your plate, and you'd see little slices of hot dog sliding around. Tonight, Amy saw, the casserole dish was surrounded by a spirit-cloud of goodness.

"How was school?" Mom asked.

"It was school," said Amy.

"Did Mrs. Barch ask if you were traumatized? She used to always ask if we were traumatized, if we had anything wrong, like a cold or a cut finger, or if you banged your head. *Anything.*"

Mrs. Barch had been a teacher when Amy's parents were in school. That's how ancient she was. At parent-teacher conferences, she asked Dad if he still had trouble remembering to zip up his pants (he did).

"Yes," said Amy. "She asked if I was traumatized."

She took a bite out of her apple.

While she was chewing, a silence happened, and Mom and Dad exchanged a peculiar look. The kind of look grown-ups sometimes exchange when they think their kids aren't watching.

Mom fidgeted with her Marie Curie ring. Something was on her mind. The ring, Amy noticed, had a faint green glow about it. She tried to ignore this.

"What am I missing?" she asked Mom, talking around her apple.

"Nothing," said Mom.

Her parents exchanged another not-so-secret look.

"You guys are very much not sly," Amy told them.

"Fine," said Dad. "It's not nothing. It's something."

Her parents still had hearts over their heads, but they had rain clouds over them. Tiny, boiling rain clouds.

The fire came to life, crackling and smoking. Dad stood up.

"We're going home, after dinner," said Mom. "We're not going to wait for the Big Duke to get here."

Dad nodded.

Amy frowned.

"It's because of me," she said. "Isn't it? Because of the

whole lightning thing. You don't think we ought to be camping out in the field here when I just got out of the hospital."

"Smart kid," said Dad. "Let's keep her."

"I don't know," said Mom. "She's getting awfully expensive. Even before the lightning—"

"It's not funny!" Amy shouted. "I'm fine! Besides, you're out here for a reason, and if you quit now—"

"It's important," Dad said. "I agree. We have to keep people from poisoning the planet just to make more money. But nothing's as important as you. You're our first responsibility. Then, maybe, saving the world."

Amy's throat tightened. Her eyes stung. She couldn't tell if she was mad or sad or grateful.

When had it become so important to her, this thing they were doing? It wasn't just an adventure, she realized. She really, really didn't want the stupid machine to tear up the ground with its stupid claw.

"Maybe," said someone, "I can be of some assistance here. Or at least make things more complicated."

A man's voice. A stranger's voice, behind them.

Amy and her parents turned to discover a man in a suit. Youngish, as grown-ups went, and sort of gawky. He wore a very neat, dark suit, with a smooth, glossy tie. In fact, he radiated neatness like a kind of sunlight. The only exception to this was his hair, which had fallen victim to the wind. It had fallen victim to *something*. His eyes, too, had something messy and unusual about them, as if they were laughing and pretending to be flashlights.

Behind the man, Amy noticed a slender black sports car parked at the roadside.

The stranger raised one gloved hand, tipped an imaginary hat, and said, "Ms. Wood, Mr. Wood, Amy Wood . . . a pleasure."

"Well—" Dad began.

"Well," interrupted the man, in the most polite way, "you were thinking of pulling up stakes. Breaking camp. Giving up the cause, et cetera, all for the good of the child. Very responsible. Very! It's what I would do, myself, as a parent."

"You have children?" asked Mom. "Mr. . . . ?"

"Not at all," answered the man. "Not ever. Who knows? But the clock is ticking, Mr. Wood, Amy Wood, Ms. Wood, as fine a family as ever there was. And I have come—at the behest of certain most excellent parties—to ask that you consider staying for one more day. Possibly two. Possibly not. It's hard to say. What do you say?"

"I'm afraid—" Dad began.

"Who isn't," interrupted the man, "at least some of the time? I know I am. Tell me you'll stay. One more day. Yes?"

"You say you represent someone," said Mom. "Who?"

"As I said," said the man, "it's hard to say."

"It's a secret," said Amy.

"We have a winner," said the man, tipping his imaginary hat a second time.

"You could be from the mining company, for all we know," said Mom.

The man rubbed his hands together as if an exciting game were being played.

"I am NOT," he said emphatically, "from, as you say, the mining company. That's not a secret at all. I am also not from the grocery store, the sky, Philadelphia, or the planet Mars. Beyond that, I am very much not at liberty to say, you see. So . . . ?"

He seemed to be expecting a reply.

If that was what he expected, Mom and Dad disappointed him.

Mom and Dad could be quite determined. They got a certain look in their eyes (which they now had) and crossed their arms over their chests (which they now did).

"Specifics," said Dad.

"If you please," said Mom, twisting her pinkie ring so fiercely that Amy worried she'd snap her finger.

The stranger's eyes got a busy, thoughtful look. His jaw worked back and forth, as if he were almost but not quite talking to himself.

"Very well," he said after a moment. "I am authorized to say this: my employers suspect the Big Duke might get here faster than everyone thinks. These huge companies don't always tell the whole truth about their plans, you know. It may well be here tomorrow at this time! If you intend to be here to carry out your protest—and I certainly hope you do!—then you mustn't retreat. You mustn't budge an inch."

"Tomorrow?" exclaimed Mom and Dad together.

"That's too soon," said Mom.

"We were hoping to have a few more days to maybe get on TV again," said Dad. "Maybe change a mind or two."

"Stay here until the machine arrives," said the stranger, "and it's quite likely you'll get on TV."

Mom and Dad still had their arms crossed. Still had that look in their eyes. They did glance at each other, though, in a surprised and worried way.

"Authorized by whom?" asked Mom.

The stranger looked puzzled.

"You said you were authorized to tell us things," said Mom. "Who authorized you? Who do you work for?"

"That," said the stranger, "must remain a secret until such and such a time."

"Tell us," insisted Dad, "or we're packing up and leaving."

The stranger, appearing resolute, said, "My deepest, most eviscerating apologies, Ms. Wood, Mr. Wood, but I can't say. I really can't. You could tie me up and threaten to lower me into a vat of hot lava, and I still couldn't tell you. I do hope you'll reconsider."

More staring. More arm crossing.

A long, not-very-friendly silence.

The man, Amy began to notice, had a peculiar haze around him. To Amy, it looked like a million Christmas lights had exploded into dust, and the dust had formed a cloud. Not unlike the Oort cloud, out in space, where comets came from. Amy liked the cloud and had a strong feeling that she should trust the man. Mr. . . . what had he said his name was?

"I think we should stay," Amy said, looking up at her mother and then her father.

And then her mother again. They weren't saying *anything*; she hated when they did that. It gave her the fidgets. They did that thing grown-ups do when they're fighting to make a tough decision, where they make a knot with their mouth and stare at something invisible in the middle of the air.

Say something! Amy screamed in her head.

But then she noticed, when the silence had gone on for three billion years, that although her parents weren't giving her any clues, the hearts over their heads kind of *were*. Both hearts kept changing shape and color, as if they were brave hearts one second and then love hearts. Blue worry hearts and thundery frustrated hearts.

It occurred to Amy that parents—even when they were totally paying attention—simply didn't know for sure what to do. And this frightened them, and they tried to hide it.

Mom's and Dad's hearts seemed to have settled on look-ing confused, as if her parents needed a hug.

So Amy hugged them. First Mom, then Dad.

There's something about a hug that says, *Things are going to be okay,* isn't there? That's how Amy thought of it. And maybe some of the okay feeling got through, because Dad looked at Mom and Amy and the stranger and said, "We'll stay."

And Mom added, "As long as she seems all right," in a nonnegotiable kind of voice.

The stranger gave a pleased little hop.

"You have made me, and certain interested parties, very happy!" he said, offering his gloved hand to be shaken. "Wheels are in motion, Ms. Wood, Mr. Wood, Amy Wood! Wheels are turning, and possibilities are brewing. I have to go tend these turnings and possibilities, and I wish you a grateful farewell."

As the odd stranger began picking his way toward the road, toward the little black sports car, Dad's face lit up with a smile.

"I get the feeling somehow," he called after the man, "that everything might turn out for the best after all."

"Possibly!" the stranger answered, hopping over an enor-mous clump of dried mud. "And quite possibly not! No harm in trying. Well, actually, perhaps a great deal of harm, but never mind. What else would I do with my time? Fix pinball machines? Have a lot of girlfriends? Knit sweaters for dogs?" And he was still talking and saying things when he passed out of earshot, reached the sports car, and sped away.

Leaving a trail of Oort cloud dust hanging over the road.

"That was strange," said Dad, squinting after the car. "And it happened very quickly."

Mom didn't say anything. She just stood there thinking things.

"I'm almost sure," said Dad, "he's from the county engineer's office. Or the university. A lot of very neat people work at the university. Have you ever noticed that?"

"Very neat," said Mom, "and in some cases very strange."

Amy, like most young people, moved on quickly.

"As long as we're staying," she said, "may I go to Moo's?"

Mom gave Amy a narrow look.

"How about we take one step at a time," she said. "You went to school, after all."

Amy started to protest but forced herself to calm down. An emotional appeal wouldn't fly too far with her parents. They were great admirers of logic and reason. So she took a few seconds to organize her thoughts and then calmly said, "I would like to present a list of raw facts."

Instantly their eyes focused and lit up.

"Say on," said Dad.

"Okay! One: you have been told by the hospital people

that I'm okay, and they're the experts. Two: if I suddenly became *not* okay—if I started to fizz like a Pepsi or develop spots like a cheetah—Moo's mom has a car, just like you do." (Amy did not actually know this for a fact, but it MUST be true? . . .) "And three: you have your smartphones, and Moo's mom has a smartphone." (Didn't she? . . .) "Plus, I did fine at school all day long and had a healthy appetite for dinner. A healthy appetite is an excellent sign that things are working well anatomically."

Mom and Dad looked impressed.

"So, please," Amy added. "Double please."

Mom and Dad traded a look.

"You're sure you feel up to it?" asked Mom.

"Uh-huh." She tried to emanate invisible waves of sureness.

"Maybe I should drive you."

Amy shook her head and said, "I really reallyreallyreally want to ride my bike, and get back to normal."

Mom was thinking it over. She was making her thinking-it-over face. The heart over her head became two hearts, and they pushed each other around.

Dad crossed his arms over his chest and said, "Maybe going to Moo's is the best possible idea."

"It's *what*?" Mom's thinking-it-over face switched to her *Are you kidding me?* face.

"In fact," Dad continued, "I'd like you to do something, if you're comfortable with it."

"'Kay," said Amy.

"Ask Moo's mom if you can stay the night."

"Really?" Amy didn't want to stay at Moo's. She wanted to come back here, to be here if anything happened with the Big Duke.

"Really?" asked Mom. She clearly wasn't on the same page as Dad. "Do you really think it's safe for your daughter-who-was-just-struck-by-lightning to spend the night away from her parents?"

"What do you suppose the chances are," said Dad, "that staying at a friend's house is more dangerous than that giant machine?"

Mom paused. The heart over her head looked like it was talking to itself for a moment. Then: "Fair enough," she said.

"Great!" said Dad. "So what do you say, Offspring? Sleepover with Moo sound good?"

"I'll see," Amy answered. "Maybe."

"I'll take it," said Dad.

"So . . . I can ride my bike there?" Amy asked.

"Fine," said Mom. "But be safe! And when you find out if you can stay the night, ask if you can call us and check in."

"Oh yeah," said Amy. "Because I can't just actually call

you on my OWN phone, because . . . let's see . . . I don't HAVE one, like a real person."

Her parents kept meaning to get her a phone, for emergencies, and they kept forgetting.

Mom rolled her eyes and kissed Amy atop the head.

Amy snugged her butterfly hoodie nice and tight, walked her bike to the road, and zoomed away.

She had no way of knowing that a bunch of VERY odd things were going to happen to her before she made it back again.

7. DEEP SCIENCE

AMY RODE THROUGH THE woods the same way she always did, as fast as possible. Just as she had expected, the woods were full of shadows. Maybe even ghosts; Amy didn't pause to investigate.

Before long she arrived at the leaning house, and there sat Moo on the porch, wearing her cow hoodie, looking at the cows over in the pasture. She didn't react at all when Amy sat down next to her and watched the cows with her.

"I got struck by lightning," Amy said.

A few seconds passed in silence.

"Look," she said, pushing her sleeves up to her elbows, displaying a pattern of dark, branchlike markings on her skin. "See that? They're called Lichtenberg figures. They explained it to me at the hospital; it's like a scar left by the lightning. They'll fade eventually."

She pulled her sleeves down again.

A slight breeze kicked up.

"Ever since I was in the hospital," Amy continued, "I've been noticing some things I hadn't noticed before, ever. Like, apparently, my mom and dad—and other people, too—have hearts over their heads. Like symbols. Like the lights on top of a cop car, except instead of saying, *Pull over!* it's like they're saying, *I love you* or *I have a good soul* or something. But there's other stuff, too. . . ."

She told about the macaroni spirit and the other things she'd seen. She took her time and told all the details she could think of. Moo wasn't going anywhere, and she never interrupted.

While Amy was talking, the breeze kicked up a little more. Some leaves blew across the yard, and across the road. Amy's eye was drawn to the sky, where gray clouds were sailing in.

Not just clouds, though. The clouds had horses in them. Gray horses with flashing eyes.

Symbol horses, Amy thought. They were what the soul of the wind looked like.

"I guess it's going to rain," she said.

Soon, she thought, she needed to ask Moo's mom if she could sleep over. Her own mom was expecting a call. But not yet.

"Anyway," she continued, "Mrs. Barch, my teacher? She had a heart over *her* head, too, but it had something wrong with it, like maybe—"

It is going to rain, said Moo. *But not for a little while.*

"Oh," said Amy. "Well, it feels like it *wants* to. Plus, there are these horses . . ."

Amy stopped talking.

"Did you *say* something just now?" she asked Moo.

She turned her head and almost jumped out of her skin. Moo was looking at her.

I said, repeated Moo, *that it's not going to rain for a while.*

Amy realized that the words, the voice, were blooming inside her head; Moo's mouth didn't move the slightest bit. Amy felt as if lightning had struck all over her insides.

"Mrrzzl!" she gasped, five times in a row.

When they run like that, said Moo, *it means it's going to be windy. If it's going to rain soon, they just stand there and float and hang their heads and look sad.*

"I don't know what to say," said Amy. "I'm in shock or

something. It's like somebody shot me with a freeze ray. You're telepathizing or doing ESP or something!"

Maybe it shouldn't be so surprising, she thought. It wasn't any stranger than macaroni spirits, or hearts over people's heads.

Moo said, *Want to walk over to the fence and see if the cows come?*

"Sure," said Amy. If Moo had said, "Want to paint ourselves bright yellow and do jumping jacks in the middle of the road?" Amy would have answered, "Sure."

Then she said, "Wait! Before we go anywhere, I'm supposed to ask you and your mom if I can sleep over. We're camping out where the Big Duke thingy is supposed to—"

I know. You told me. They're being all protective. That would be awesome! Ask Mom.

Amy jumped up to knock on the door.

Amy?

Moo was giving her a serious look.

"Yep?"

Don't mention anything about the talking and telepathizing.

"I wasn't going to."

And she knocked, and Moo's mom ghosted her way to the door and said yes, of course she could stay, if it was okay that they had only cornflakes for breakfast, and yes, Amy could use her phone, and Amy called Mom and gave the phone back and said, "Thanks."

"Excellent," she said, hopping off the porch, then turning to face Moo, who agreed that it was excellent.

Amy took Moo by the elbow and pulled, and Moo stood.

They walked across the yard, looked both ways, crossed the street, and waited by the fence.

Moo yelled, "MOO!"

Some cows mooed back and plodded in their direction.

These cows are the most free, most happy cows in the whole world, declared Moo.

That was probably true, Amy thought.

"What made you decide to talk to me?" she asked.

I've ALWAYS talked to you, said Moo. *You just couldn't hear me till now.*

"I didn't think you even *could* talk!"

Well, said Moo, *I can and I can't. I do and I don't. I can talk to you in your head because the lightning opened up your brain or your soul or something. But I can't talk out loud. Maybe someday. And I can't write. I can read still, and understand what people say, but I can't make words. I hate it. It's like being tied up with duct tape.*

Amy frowned. She reached over and gave Moo's shoulder a squeeze.

The wind quickened. Overhead, the horses' hooves were a speeding blur. Amy's hair flew behind her like a flag.

"MooOOOOOooooOOOoo!" said the cows, arriving at the fence.

This whole thing was so exciting! She couldn't get over it: Moo could TALK! They could be like real friends now! Amy wanted to cry and laugh and jump up and down. Her whole self wanted to BOING like a rubber band.

Go ahead, said Moo.

"Go ahead what?"

BOING all over the place. It's wonderful! I'm happy, too! I'm just not the BOINGing type.

"You can hear inside my head," said Amy, clapping her hands over her mouth.

Amy, asked Moo, *don't you get it?*

"Yes," said Amy. "Get what?"

It's not just me. It's YOU, too! Don't you GET it? You can see and hear now the way I can. Say something.

"Something," said Amy, trembling.

Dur, said Moo. *Without using your regular voice.*

Once upon a time, Amy thought, *there were three little pigs.*

Something original, maybe. Really? Three little pigs?

Oh my God. Amy's eyes stung, and out leaked a single tear. They were telepathizing! This was wonderful, wonderful!

Yes, said Moo. *It's wonderful. Everything is about eighty thousand times more wonderful than you ever dreamed. EVERYTHING. Before, you could see only the surface of the world; now you can see it all.*

"Look at the clouds!" said Amy, pointing at the horses.

You don't have to actually speak, Loud Girl.

"Loud Girl?"

It's a nickname I called you in my head. You know . . . before you could hear me.

"Well . . . it's not very nice."

It's not any not-nicer than Moo, if you think about it.

"You wear a cow costume every second of your life. You moo at the cows."

It's okay. I like it. My real name is Gertrude June Kopernikus.

"Well, call me Amy, not Loud Girl. Anyway, I think I like talking out loud. It's what I'm used to."

Amy.

"MOOooooOOO," said the cows, getting impatient to have their noses rubbed and some grass handed to them through the fence.

The cows had little symbolic trees growing on their backs, and green fields and warm sunlight.

"It's like the cows are miniature planet Earths," said Amy, amazed.

Yep, said Moo. *Everything has some kind of spirit. Or theme. Or whatever you want to call it. Look around harder.*

Moo was right.

The grass underfoot was still grass, but Amy saw that it glowed in a way she'd never noticed before, as if she could discern life running through it. The rough fence under her hands remembered being a tree.

Not far from Amy's left foot lay a smooth gray stone. The stone was old and sleeping, she saw. The stone remembered being born way down deep, where the earth was a giant furnace.

It was too much! Amy squeezed her eyes closed.

"What IS it?" she asked in a small voice, beginning to be a bit frightened. "These things we can see. Talking between our minds. Are we possessed?"

Don't be silly, answered Moo. *It's a kind of science, just like the forces that make the grass grow and gravity happen. People just don't understand it yet. It's like Deep Science. That's how I think of it.*

"Deep Science?"

Remember in The Lion, the Witch and the Wardrobe *how they had normal magic, and then there was the Deep Magic?*

"Yeah."

Same idea, except with science. Deep Science kinda looks like magic 'cause we don't know how it works yet. I think what's happening is that the universe tries to talk to us, in a way. It sends us symbols and makes its thoughts visible, but not everybody can see them yet. Something has to happen that changes your brain.

Moo, Amy noticed, had a little glowing cow grazing in the air atop her head.

Let's go over the fence, said Moo. *I've never been in the pasture.*

"I don't think *anyone* goes there," said Amy. Did Moo know about the witch? The witch who had eaten children?

Everyone knows about the witch, said Moo. *Besides, I didn't say, 'Let's go in the woods.' I just want to go over, into the field. I'm dying to go SOMEWHERE.*

So Amy put one foot on the lowest rail and reached for Moo's elbow, nudging.

Moo followed. One foot up, two feet up, one leg over, then the other, and they were there, in the tickly long weeds on the far side, on the cow side.

The cows watched as the girls held hands and ran off through the—

I'm not really the running type.

—as the girls walked off through the grass and stones, through the twilight and the wind.

8. SHE HIT HIM WITH A SAUCEPAN

THE PAIR CROSSED THE field in a roundabout way that led farther from the fence but no closer to the woods.

Moo paused, bent, and retrieved something from the ground.

"Whatdjuh find?" asked Amy.

Moo opened her hand, displaying two rugged gray stones.

Take one, she said, so Amy did.

You must have brought me a hundred stones and rocks by

now, said Moo. *Today it's my turn. These are my official "The Day I Found Someone to Talk To" stones.*

Amy sort of wanted to cry. Moo had noticed and appreciated all the various dumb things she had done. It was wonderful to know.

They dropped the stones into their hoodie pockets and continued walking.

"I remember when you came to school," said Amy.

School, said Moo darkly.

Amy understood. Sometimes she, too, felt dark about school. But it was interesting sometimes. Like in third grade, when her class had put some eggs in an incubator and they'd hatched into chicks.

No one did anything like that the day I was there, said Moo. *They mostly just stared at me. Mom keeps saying she's going to give it another try, but so far . . .*

They hopped over a cow patty so fresh it was steaming.

"Moo," said Amy, "what happened? How come you can't talk, or move on your own?"

(She surprised herself, asking this. Wasn't sure she *should* ask.)

I don't want to talk about it, answered Moo.

"Sorry." (Yep. Shouldn't have asked.) "Sometimes my mouth gets out there and says things before I can think them over. Especially with questions. It's part of being a scientist. Being professionally nosy."

They hopped over a log together, counting *One, two, three* as they did.

It's okay, said Moo. *You're nice.*

"I'm not that nice. I steal things."

I know. I've been listening to you for days and months and maybe a year now.

Moo must think she talked too much.

No, said Moo. *It's my favorite thing in the world.*

Moo pulled at Amy's hand, bringing them both to a stop.

I changed my mind, she said. *I'll tell you.*

"Only if it's really all right. Like, really, really triple-*truly* all right. I don't want you to feel like—"

Shhhh, said Moo, squeezing her hand.

Then she pulled her hand free and crossed her arms over her chest as she walked.

They passed a gopher hole and a smelly puddle where a cow had peed.

My mom used to live here, said Moo, *a long time ago, when she was little. And she liked it a lot. But when she got older, she met my father.*

Pause. They walked around a thistle bush growing all by itself.

You know how some people think they're right about everything, all the time? He was like that. He thought they should move to another city, far away, so they did. He thought they should live in this one house, so they did. He wanted to have an artificial Christmas tree and watch this show or that show on TV, and they always did what he wanted. Then I was born. I don't think having a daughter was something he wanted, but that's one thing he didn't get to choose.

Moo sounded like she was spitting the words out.

But he wasn't just pushy and selfish. He was mean. He got mad so easy, over nothing. Like he had secret buttons, and if you accidentally pushed one, he turned into almost another person. So he used to hit Mom. I think he tried to do it when I wasn't in the room, but you know how it is—kids see waaaay more than grown-ups think. They think we're a little bit stupid, so it's like we have the gift of invisibility sometimes. Anyway, Mom would put up her arms around her head and stay totally quiet and just kind of wait for him to be done.

Amy's eyes stung. She had never known that it could be difficult just to *hear* something. It scared her. She knew that not everyone's mom and dad were like her mom and dad, but hearing about it for real was something new. She didn't like it. She wrapped her arms around herself like a bear hug.

They walked in silence for a bit, making their way across the pasture like a couple of brewing storms. The second time they encountered a thistle bush, they stomped right over it.

And then one day he hit me.

I don't think he was planning on it. I mean, I don't think he ever planned on hitting, but he especially didn't plan on hitting me. I think he understood, in his pushy, selfish brain, that hitting his little kid was more . . . more wrong than he wanted to be. Like he could stand to be someone who hit my mom, but not someone who beat up his kid. You know?

No, Amy *didn't* know. Amy wanted to run away. But she didn't, and she didn't say anything, either. Tried not to even think anything.

I'm sorry, said Moo. *I'll stop. I'm hurting you.*

"No!" said Amy, surprising herself again. Staring straight ahead, stomping straight ahead, she softly repeated, "No," and said nothing more.

They were in the kitchen, and she pushed one of his secret buttons . . . like she made him a baloney sandwich and he wanted ham or something, and I came in while he was hitting her. And I ran up and shoved him. Which must have pushed about a hundred secret buttons, and he sort of exploded. I'm not sure what happened then. . . . My head hit the refrigerator, I know that. I don't remember anything else until later, when I woke up at the hospital. When I woke up and couldn't make words and couldn't move myself unless someone helped me, like being tied up to a chair inside my own body. But I know what happened next, because Mom told me.

Moo was crying, and had sped up. Walking faster and talking faster, as if trying to finish her story and also somehow outrun it.

When Mom saw him hit me, she snapped. She picked up a saucepan and hit him in the head. HARD. And then she called an ambulance and the cops. And later when they saw that I couldn't talk and couldn't move, they put my dad in jail. And my mom moved us back here. And you know the rest. So there you go.

They stomped for a while longer. Amy noticed that they had, for some reason, gone in a big circle. You could see a circle in the pasture where they had left footprints and flat spots.

Moo seemed to run low on gas. She slowed and then stopped.

Looking at her for the first time since the story began, Amy saw that Moo was still crying, but not with actual tears. Her eyes were as distant and weird as ever, but Amy could feel the crying happening *inside* her.

She threw her arms around Moo and squeezed her like a boa constrictor.

Mom thinks it's all her fault, said Moo. And I can't argue about it with her. She can't hear me, and I can't make words on paper any more than with my mouth.

Amy squeezed harder. She wanted to tell Moo that it was all right. That's what you were supposed to tell people, wasn't it? But it wasn't all right. So she just hugged.

I think, said Moo, that you are smooshing my liver.

Amy loosened up.

I'm not so much into hugging.

Amy stood back and stepped in a cow patty but didn't care. She could still hear the story whirling around in Moo's head, winding down. How Moo's mom's hair had gotten gray, and she seemed to turn gray inside, too. How the doctors had said Moo might start moving on her own again someday or might not, but she probably wouldn't be able to talk again. How Moo's mom had taken Moo to school that one time but had been told it was no use, no use.

No use.

Overhead in the sky, the horses hung their heads.

It began to rain ever so slightly.

And then harder.

They pulled their hoods up over their heads and stood looking at each other—a cow and a butterfly in the middle of the pasture.

We have to go into the woods, said Moo.

WHAT?! thought Amy. *You don't go into the woods! Hello? The witch?*

Well, we can't just stay out here getting poured on and saturated. We'll get pneumonia or diarrhea or something. We can just go into the edge part of the woods.

"But—"

I'm pretty sure that witches live in the deep parts of the woods, not at the edges.

It made sense. And the rain was getting awfully wet and

cold. Amy thought she could feel some pneumonia starting to stir down in her lung. Or her lungs.

"MOOooooOOOOooo!" said the cows, some distance away, and Amy saw that they were moving out of the pasture. Amy had read that it was often a smart thing to pay attention to what animals did.

Still! It was getting late. She could feel it getting late.

Amy found herself worrying about her parents. Maybe Moo's story had put her mind in worry mode. She hated the idea of them sitting in the dark, on top of the red X, with that awful, stupid machine creeping up on them, faster and faster. A LOT faster, if it was going to be there in less than a day. Her heart started knocking on her ribs as if it wanted out. At the same time, everything that was happening was like a strange, wild wind blowing through her life, promising to take her places and show her things if she would allow it.

Amy? said Moo. *I'm starting to have symptoms of the Black Death from the Medieval Ages, I think. Let's go!*

Amy went. A thrill of excitement electrified her skin.

The girls held hands and headed for the woods.

9. LOST

A FUNNY THING HAPPENS when it rains in the woods. It doesn't rain at first, because the rain stops and pitty-pats around on the leaves, way overhead. So you can hear it, but you can't feel it yet, and everything stays dry for a minute or two.

Then the rain starts to find its way in, first dropping from leaf to leaf and finally plunging down among the bushes and dead gunk on the forest floor, and the sound it makes is this great big enormous SIGH, as if the woods were breathing.

The girls stopped and sat down under a tree about a hundred steps inside the woods just as the water started dripping down through the leaves.

Amy said, "It's going to get really dark soon. Is your mom going to freak?"

Moo shrugged. *Not necessarily. She goes to bed really early. . . . It's like she spends her whole life being tired and depressed. It's almost her job. . . . So if we get back kinda late, she might not even know.*

"Well, we should definitely go back when it quits raining."

It got visibly darker while they were having this conversation.

"Whoa," said Amy. "It got darker."

The rain got wetter.

"Are you afraid of the dark?" Amy asked. "I am."

I know.

"What do you mean, 'I know'?"

You wrote me a poem about it one time. It went like this:

I'm afraid of the dark and the night.
Who knows what goes on when you turn off the
    light?

Amy waited.

That's all, said Moo. *It wasn't very long. Or very good.*

Amy might have been slightly offended, but she had other things on her mind. She could *feel* things around them in the dark. . . .

There ARE things around us in the dark, said Moo.

"There are not! Like what?"

Ghosts.

It got completely dark just then. The dark almost went THUMP—that's how sudden and complete it was.

Amy jumped and yelped.

Shhhh, said Moo. *Calm down. Not like Halloween ghosts.*

"There's another kind?"

Uh-huh. How can I explain it? Things are older in the woods than they are in your bedroom or at school. The woods have been here longer. They have dreams and memories that kind of float around. Like ghosts.

"What kind of dreams and memories?"

The rain came down harder, in huge, splashy drops.

Like, right where we're sitting? said Moo. *A deer died once. And all through the woods, there was a fire a long time ago. Plus, the new trees remember the old trees, and they remember when they were seeds and acorns. Right now the rain is making the woods remember other times it rained.*

Amy felt better. Sort of. Not really.

She realized suddenly that she could see Moo hunched beside her. Not clearly.

A light, over in the trees.

Ghosts! thought Amy.

The moon, said Moo.

And so it was.

"So beautiful," said Amy, yawning.

Beautiful, agreed Moo, yawning because Amy yawned.

They fell asleep watching it rise through the trees.

WHEN AMY WOKE UP, she found herself in another world.

A world made of fog.

But what a fog! Morning sunlight diffused into a glow, as if the woods had filled up with wool. If someone shrank you to the size of a flea and set you down on the back of the world's fluffiest sheep, it would be just like this fog.

OMG! Memories of everything that had happened came flooding back to her.

Moo had spoken! Rain! The woods! Ghosts!

"HOLY COW!" she cried.

Moo, next to her, opened one eye and said, *Loud Girl.*

"If I don't get back at *some* point," said Amy, "my parents will think I've been abducted. They'll call the air force."

This was not actually likely, she knew. Her parents loved her to death, but they were soooooo absentminded. They might notice she was late, or they might not. They had a lot on their minds.

"I have to get back to see what happens with the Big Duke," she said.

She told Moo about the strange man in the suit who had urged them not to quit and go home. "As if something important and unexpected was going to happen."

Moo nodded. She seemed to understand about important and unexpected things.

Amy bit her lip and frowned. "There's more to it, though," she said. "I'm not sure how to explain it. My mom and dad connect with the world in *big* ways, like knowing we have to stop messing up the earth, but then sometimes they miss obvious, simpler stuff. I think I'm supposed to be there . . . to help make sure they don't miss something. I don't know what. It's like these vision thingies we can see; I can't explain it yet, but it's real. If I'm not there, something bad might happen."

Well, said Moo, *I have two things to say. One: it does sound like you should be there. And two: there's no reason you can't be. It's early. Isn't it?*

The two of them stood together, separately considering the fog.

Amy glanced down and discovered that a pool of water had collected between two mighty roots. Her reflection—her parallel-dimension self—looked up at her from this pool.

"It probably *is* early still," said Self. "But do you know which way to go to get out of the woods?"

"Of course," Amy answered, pointing. "It's that way."

Self looked skeptical.

"Or," said Amy, "maybe that way. It's definitely that way, this way, or that way there."

Uh-oh. Mrrzzl.

What, asked Moo, *are you doing?*

"Um. Arguing with my reflection. Myself in a parallel dimension. It's a habit. I do it when I'm nervous."

Well, stop. It's weird. We have each other to argue with now.

"This is true." It *was* true, Amy thought. How nice.

Are you arguing about which way is home?

"Maybe."

Well, I can't tell; can you?

"I don't suppose you can, like, see the *spirit* of the way we came, or sense which way your house is?"

What, like a lighthouse?

"Yeah."

Moo appeared to be thinking.

Maybe, she said after a moment. *Not sure. I have, after all, been mostly sitting on the porch for two years.*

She appeared to think some more.

That way, she said, pointing. *On a scale of one to a*

hundred, I'm ninety-four percent sure this is the way back toward my house.

And the funny thing was, Amy thought she could feel it, too. Every direction looked the same (foggy), but this particular way had a kind of glow to it. A kind of *THIS WAY* feeling. A 94 percent feeling.

So she said "'Kay," and took Moo by the hand and gently pulled—

Wait, said Moo. *Let go of my hand.*

Moo's voice had an odd tone to it. Amy let her go.

I want to see something, said Moo.

She stood there silently for a moment.

"You're trying to move on your own," said Amy. "Aren't you?"

Moo nodded and said, *Shhhh.*

More silence. Then Moo said, *I think I remember doctors telling Mom that I might be able to get my own movement back someday. I kind of thought, with me following you around as much as I've been doing, maybe something had shaken loose.*

"And?"

Moo shook her head. *Not yet.*

She sounded disappointed but not defeated.

Amy took her hand again and gave a little tug, and they climbed together over a fallen tree that they didn't remember climbing over on the way in.

"I kind of think I should remind you," said Amy, "that these aren't just any old woods."

Kids got eaten here, answered Moo. *I know.*

Rain began to hiss down through the leaves.

Thunder rumbled. Amy wondered how far away. If she were to see a lightning flash, she would count. (The idea of lightning didn't appeal to her very much.)

They passed through a clearing and around a huge, mossy rock. They stopped to throw stones in a small, dark pond. Amy didn't recall having passed the pond. She had a feeling she would have remembered it; the water, like wind and stone, had a theme. Not something she could see. It was something she heard. Or almost heard, the way you almost hear a train sometimes, far away.

Thunder again. Closer? Hard to tell.

I think maybe I have more of a fifty-two percent feeling, Moo admitted.

"It still feels like the right way, though," whispered Amy. "Right?"

I guess, Moo whispered back, in a 40 percent kind of way.

The rain came down harder, and it was colder than before.

We need a tree, said Moo. *A big one, with big leaves, that will act like an umbrella.*

FLASH! Lightning strobed the woods.

"One one thousand," Amy counted, "two one thousand—"

BOOM! A stout thunderclap! *RuuUUMMBle . . . !*

"Lightning," said Amy, in a voice like a mouse.

So maybe not a tree, said Moo. *Lightning likes trees. Maybe something more like a big rock to hide under.*

Amy tried to use her spirit-vision (that's how she thought of it) to zero in on a big rock, but it didn't seem to be working—

Over there, said Moo.

"A tree?"

No. Something . . .

Amy saw it, too.

It was a house.

A dark little house, looming in the fog, with waterfalls of rain splashing from its old, sagging roof.

Immediately Amy thought, *THAT'S WHERE THE WITCH LIVES!* and came THIS CLOSE to peeing herself. Not that it would have mattered; they were pretty much soaked by the rain.

I'm not sure anyone lives there, said Moo. *It looks kind of past tense.*

True.

But, said Moo, *it'll be drier in there. Probably.*

"It will also be gross and dark, and possibly a witch lives there."

Moo gave Amy a searching look.

If you really think about it, she said, *I mean reeeeeeally think, honestly, do you seriously believe there's an actual witch?*

Amy reeeeeally thought about it.

Possibly not, she admitted. Kids had disappeared, according to Dad. But that was a long time ago. And she was old enough to know how stories behaved, growing larger with time.

Besides, she reeeeeally wanted to be someplace dry. And what if there was someone inside who was friendly and helpful?

She gave the house a thoughtful look. A brave look.

It reminded Amy of Moo's house, in a way, because it didn't sit up straight. The only thing holding it upright, in fact, was a tree. A tree grew up one side, hugging the house with branches and roots. Beneath the largest branch, a door opened like a mouth.

The girls hesitated.

FLASH! *BOOM! RUUUUUUMMMMMMMBLE!*

They shot through the door, into darkness.

10. A CLOCK FROM THE GEORGE WASHINGTON DC TIMES

AT FIRST, BEFORE THEIR eyes adjusted, the girls could only tell that the house had one room and that it was . . . full. Not packed-from-floor-to-ceiling full, like a storage room, but full in the way a house is full when a busy and interesting person has lived there.

There was, for example (their dark-adjusting eyes discerned), a row of old kettles and teapots on a shelf above a fireplace. A picture of a cow, framed and faded. A bookshelf full of books, all swollen and discolored. A statue of an Egyptian cat goddess, some Chinese paper lanterns hanging from ruined beams, an oilcan, a vacuum cleaner, some wine bottles, an old radio with an enormous silver dial, a little bronze rabbit the size of a Ping-Pong ball, a cardboard box full of Legos—

"Score!" cried Amy.

—a tool bench with tools on it, and a rocking chair. A framed, faded picture of a majestic black bird. A cardboard box full of what looked like buttons, a number of discarded snake skins, a string of rusty cowbells—

Score! cried Moo.

—a pile of old record albums, an unusually large birdcage, a stone fireplace with logs in it, the skulls of a number of small animals, a tall wooden clock with a door in the front, a cloudy glass jar with something horrible in it, and a hand-painted china platter featuring a partridge in a pear tree.

Over this whole collection, a leaky roof splashed and dribbled and plinked and plunked.

Amy and Moo surveyed these things, imagining what kind of person lived like this and wondering if that person was a witch.

Whoever it is, said Moo, *they like cows. How bad could they be?*

"I guess so," said Amy. A huge raindrop blooped down right on the tip of her nose and made her face twitch.

The clock, said Moo.

"What about it?"

Bring me over there.

They drifted across the floor, and Moo stared at the clock as if hypnotized. Amy was unsurprised to find the clockface, hands and all, practically ablaze with pulsing green light.

It's old, said Moo. *Seriously old, like from the George Washington DC times.*

"You see the green, right? I think it's—"

It's time. It flows and surrounds things, just like fire or water.

"I *knew* it!"

The clock was a fabulous piece of work. Fancy lines and leaves and scrolls had been carved into the cabinet, surrounding painted scenes from faraway lands: sea dragons and mystical gardens, swordsmen in turbans, and fire-eaters floating on clouds. The panels curved out as if the clock had swallowed a beach ball. The face itself, beneath the green halo, appeared undamaged and was etched with a pair of caterpillars smoking cigars.

Amy reached out to touch it.

Maybe you shouldn't, said Moo too late.

Amy's finger pierced the light, provoking soft, bright ripples.

She brushed the minute hand with her thumb.

The clockface changed.

Changed how?

At first Amy thought the face shrank. Or did it grow larger? It turned pink! No, it filled with stars.

"Oh!" she gasped, withdrawing her hand. A tiny green cloud clung to her thumb for a moment, like a glowing tentacle, as if she had disturbed a tiny luminescent octopus.

The tentacle faded and fell away. The girls backed up a step.

"This is the most wonderful experiment of all time," Amy whispered.

This is witchy, said Moo. *That's what it is. Aw, man . . . the roof just leaked a big one right on my head!*

They looked at the clock for a minute. Amy felt the clock looking back at them. If this was an experiment, she thought, what exactly should they try to learn? What form should the experiment take?

RuuuummMMMmmble! Outside, the thunder seemed to have put some distance behind it. The plinks and plunks of the leaky roof backed off, too.

"I want to try something," she said.

Be careful, said Moo, who of course already knew what she had in mind.

Amy raised her hand to the clockface again. This time, ever so gingerly, she gave the hour hand a push.

Just like before, the face turned pink (or purple?) and spun (or sang).

The hour hand moved, with a faint creak, from the 3 to the 4.

Moo made a surprised noise, out loud.

Amy stepped back, shaking green time tendrils from her finger.

"Well," she said.

Moo was looking at her with HUGE, giant, surprised eyes.

You didn't see it, she said, *did you?*

"I saw the clock act funny."

EVERYTHING acted funny! I can't believe you didn't SEE! Oh my God! Amy . . . the light changed and the shadows moved!

"Okay," said Amy.

Well, um . . . I think we went forward an hour.

It sounded impossible.

"Impossible," Amy said.

But it was brighter now inside the house, and the shadows *were* different.

Goose bumps paralyzed her. Icy spiders crawled down her spine.

"Moo," she squeaked, "things like this don't really happen."

I agree, except, quite obviously, they do. (Moo's voice sounded shaky.)

They exchanged stares with the clock again.

Move it back, said Moo.

Amy gulped and set the hour hand back where it had been. This time she was careful to watch the rocking chair, which cast a sharp shadow across the dusty floorboards.

The shadow grew longer. The house darkened a bit. At the edge of Amy's vision, other shadows moved, too.

Both girls choked back screams. Amy took Moo by the arm and marched her outside. She sat the two of them down in some wet leaves beside the door, where they stayed with their mouths hanging open until a bug landed on Amy's lip.

"Blech!" she spat.

The rain, at least, had found somewhere else to go. Amy listened for thunder. Heard only birds and a soft wind in the high leaves.

I think I know, said Moo, *what the experiment should be. What we should do.*

"Yes?"

We could turn the clock back a few hours and I could still get home before my mom wakes up to make cornflakes. And not worry her, and not be in trouble.

Amy nodded.

"We *could* go straight back," she said. "On the other hand, there are lots of other interesting things we could do."

Moo's forehead wrinkled. *I thought,* she said, *you needed to get back and help your parents fight the mining company, because of what the weird stranger said, and—*

"I *do*," said Amy. "But that's the wonderful thing about time travel. . . . It doesn't matter when you *leave,* as long as you go *back* to the right time. We could sit around for a month eating cheese sticks and still get back before dark-thirty yesterday. Except instead of eating cheese sticks—"

We could go back and see dinosaurs, said Moo.

"We could go back and see the Romans."

We could go forward and see if the earth gets wiped out by floods and radiation.

"We could go forward and see floating cities and flying cars."

We could spy on ourselves in the future and see if we're millionaires or in prison.

"We could see if people learn to escape their bodies and take forms like fire or soap bubbles."

I want to see when the cows first came to the woods, said Moo.

"Oh yeah, right, out of all the things you POSSIBLY could see!"

But Moo was serious.

I'm serious, she said.

"Okay. I know. But listen: I think there might be a problem."

Lovely. What?

"Well, when we turned the hour hand one hour, it moved us in time one hour."

Mmm-hmm.

"Think how long it would take to stand there and turn the hands enough to go back years. Even one year. And my dad says the cows have been here since he was a teenager."

A few moments passed. A woodpecker drilled somewhere up in the trees—*knockknockknockknockknockknock knockknockknock!*—and the drilling echoed.

After a while, Moo said, *Let's go back inside.*

"Okay. Why?"

I want to see something.

"All right."

Amy took Moo's arm, and back into the house they went. As their eyes adjusted, Amy looked around as if looking for something in particular. Looked at the teapots, the china platter, the cowbells, the horrible thing in the jar. . . .

There. The box of buttons. Look at it real hard.

They both looked hard at the buttons.

The buttons glowed, Amy noticed, just slightly. Like the clock, but not nearly as bright.

The time stuff, said Moo. *It's on other things, too. I'll bet it's on everything!*

"Except maybe some things more than others. Like things that belonged to people. Things that have stories."

Amy reached into the box of buttons and dug around until she found (felt, actually) what she was looking for. A beautiful button, big enough for someone to wear on a necklace, say, or a really big ring. An ivory cameo with a tiny portrait of a woman. Green light flickered around its edges.

Amy took Moo's hand and dropped the ring into her palm.

"Maybe someone wore this at her wedding," she said.

Moo turned the cameo over and over in her hands.

Maybe, she said, *someone wore it when she was murdered.*

"Or when she learned to fly an airplane."

Or when she murdered someone.

"Dark much? Maybe it belonged to the czarina of Russia. Maybe it was lost for years at the bottom of the sea and then found again by treasure hunters. Anyhow, the same could be true of anything in here."

Okay, so we look for things that have stories, even though we can never know what those stories are, and gather them together around the clock—

"And they make, basically, FUEL for making time go back and forth. The more stuff you have—"

STORY stuff!

"—the faster and better the clock can move around in time."

The girls looked each other in the eye.

Bizarre, said Moo.

Amy shrugged. "All great experiments seem bizarre at first," she declared. "This is the deepest science of all!"

Moo frowned.

What if the clock takes us somewhere, she said, *or some-when, and then quits being deeply scientific and leaves us stranded in 1925 or some terrible time before there was television?*

They looked each other in the eye.

"I don't know," said Amy. "Shall we do it anyway?"

Outside, up in the trees, the woodpecker drilled again. *Knockknockknockknockknockknockknockknockknock . . .*

We shall, said Moo.

11. SOMETHING LIKE A ROCKING GARAGE SALE

HOW ODD.

How simple it can be, building a time machine, when you can see the things that have time in them, like a vein of gold in a mine.

Like the tiny bronze rabbit Amy and Moo discovered, which turned out to be a bell (which had belonged to an old man who was stuck in a wheelchair, who rang the bell when he needed something).

Like the something horrible floating in the jar (I won't tell you what it is; it's too horrible).

Like some dolls they found in an old rolltop desk (dolls made of linen and corn husks, which had been carried across mountains by a family escaping war).

Like a box full of baby teeth. Like a moldy book of poems. Like snake skins and teapots and cowbells.

Like the rocking chair (which had gone up inside a Kansas tornado in 1975, carrying Mrs. Hannah P. Stafford and her cat, Mr. Goose; chair and cat had come down safely, but Mrs. Stafford had not, seemingly, come down at all).

And of course the clock (once owned and lovingly wound by Eleanor Roosevelt), and of course the ivory cameo (owned by and buried with Eleanor Roosevelt and recovered when her grave was robbed . . . which hardly anyone knows about but you, and you mustn't tell).

The girls also found some wire, which wasn't storied or full of time but was quite perfect for attaching all these things to the rocking chair, until the chair was transformed into something like a rocking museum or garage sale. It glowed and hummed as if it disliked sitting still and wished to be off someplace.

The sunlight and shadows had changed meantime. Not because of Deep Science, but because of the very ordinary science of a morning going by.

It did occur to Amy that if someone lived here, the probability of that someone's coming home increased with every minute, and what would that person think of two girls doing fantastical things to the rocking chair, and what if that person turned out to be a witch after all? Only a witch, she was sure, could possibly live in a rotting, leaking ruin like this, interesting though it might be.

If someone were coming, said Moo, *we'd hear them marching through the woods. Through all the leaves and sticks and things.*

Probably true. Amy kept an ear tuned, monitoring the woods like radar.

It also occurred to her, and troubled her, that somewhere out there the Big Duke was rumbling and crawling toward her parents. She had to keep reminding herself how important their experiment was to science (*Deep* Science!), and how even if it didn't work, they could always just use the clock to go back to this morning.

Stop worrying, said Moo, *and work. Take this wire. Tie this cowbell so it hangs under the birdcage. Excellent. . . .*

IT MAY HAVE BEEN lunchtime by the time Amy and Moo stood back to consider their work.

"If nothing else," said Amy, "it makes a nice sculpture."

How do we make it go? asked Moo. *How do we make it stop?*

"We make it go by ringing the little rabbit bell," said Amy. "I don't know how we make it stop. But I think it will just know when the right time is. It will be guided by our thoughts or something."

How do you know?

"I don't," said Amy, sitting down in the rocking chair, pulling Moo with her.

It was a largish rocking chair. The girls fit in side by side, just barely, if they squooshed.

I want to ring the bell, said Moo.

"So do I," said Amy.

They rang the bell together.

Nothing happened.

Fudge, said Moo.

Great. Just great. It occurred to Amy that they had made an awful lot of assumptions about what the chair and the time stuff might or might not do, and now, of course, they were a million times later than before, and—

An idea fizzed in her brain.

"I might know why," she said.

Moo was listening.

"Ever since you told me about the ghosts, the memories of the woods, I've noticed that some places seem more . . . *lively* than others."

Lively?

"Spiritier. Ghostier. Like the pond where we threw stones. We learned in science that water is really, really old. It never goes away; it just changes form, from steam or ice or liquid or rain or slime or pee or—"

So we should take the chair thing to the pond, and the pond will act like a time catapult?

Amy shrugged. "Maybe. Of course, if someone lives here, they might not appreciate us burglarizing things out of their house."

Borrowing, said Moo. *We'll bring it back.*

True. Amy understood this logic perfectly, as an experienced crime scientist.

She rocked the chair a little.

"It's *heavy*," she observed.

Moo shrugged. *The pond wasn't that far back,* she said. *It's, like, just downhill.*

Amy shrugged. "Okay," she said.

It took them a moment to figure out how to get a grip on the clock machine thing, but then Moo threw her arms around the clock, and Amy lifted the rocking chair runners as if pushing a wheelbarrow, and together they staggered out the door. Once amid the wet leaves at the top of the hill, they found that their invention behaved not unlike a sleigh. With very little trouble, they nursed it down between trees and around a couple of rocks to the edge of the pond. Easy. Almost as if the clock chair *wanted* to be there.

As they arrived, the fog seemed to thin, unveiling the dark water.

The water didn't glow green. It vibrated, though, with a wild, ancient hum. Amy could feel it more than she felt anything else, including her own skin and bones, as if everything else were a daydream, and the water were the only thing real and wide awake.

They took a minute to catch their breath, then climbed aboard the chair.

Immediately Amy popped back off and went crouching along the edge of the pond, looking for something. She reached into the shallowest part of the water and was back aboard the chair in an instant, a flat brown stone in each hand.

"Here," she said, handing one stone to Moo.

"For luck," she said.

Wait! exclaimed Moo. *Not just luck. Look!*

The stones in their palms glowed, in an old, dreamy way.

"Extra fuel," said Amy.

They dropped the stones into their pockets.

By silent agreement, both girls pulled their hoods up, snugged the laces tight. They nodded at each other, and their ears and horns and antennae bounced up and down.

They rang the bell together.

Say "Moooooo!" said Moo.

"Why?"

So it'll know we want to stop at the time when the wild cows came to the woods.

"Mooooooo!" Amy mooed.

Mooooooo! mooed Moo.

The chair jerked beneath them then. Its green aura gave a throb, and it shook, as if gathering itself to leap, to somersault, to fly, to—

But something else was happening, too, Amy sensed. She was puzzled, and she frowned.

You have to concentrate, said Moo. *What is it?*

"Listen!" said Amy.

Her radar ears had finally heard the thing she'd been afraid of hearing. Someone crunching and snapping and striding through twigs and leaves. Someone who quite suddenly appeared over the top of the hill.

A witch.

"Moo!" Amy cried.

Amy! cried Moo.

The witch—what else could she be? (she was scary and old and dressed in black, and was waving old, long, hooked fingers, phantom eyes blazing)—came loping downhill, straight at them.

Amy threw up in her mouth just the slightest bit.

"NooooOOOoOooooo!" the witch was screaming.

Screaming with an awful mouth big enough to eat a kid. "NooOOOOOOOOOOO!"

"Go!" hollered Amy, shaking the chair with her hands, crying, thinking, *Oh my GOD, I can't believe she's real!*

Then, suddenly, something else was happening.

Something else that couldn't be real.

About ten feet away, the air exploded in a green FLASH, and Amy saw . . .

Saw herself and Moo, and the chair and the clock and everything, come flying out of nowhere and go crashing and smashing through the leaves and gunk along the edge of the pond. Saw it all come apart, tumbling like popcorn—chair, knickknacks, clock, girls—and blur to a stop, mostly in pieces.

Moo—the *other* Moo, the one who had just arrived out of nowhere—sat up and looked at them, and they looked at her.

They looked at Amy, too. But the Amy who had just come cannonballing out of thin air did not look back at them or sit up or anything.

Her head and hair were bright with blood, and she wasn't moving.

Amy felt her whole self go cold.

And then the witch had them.

Sharp, clawlike hands reached for the clock chair, reached for Moo's arm, and—

"GO!" wailed both girls, clenching their whole minds and bodies and hearts and fists and—

A wild green *WHOOOOOOSH* erased everything, swallowed everything, became everything. . . .

THE WHOOSH GAVE WAY to something like a time-lapse movie.

Inside the movie, the light changed.

Shadows turned, moving with the sun. The sun itself hurried overhead, shooting sunbeams down through the leaves.

"OMG," said Amy. "It's working, it's working, it's working."

Her words stretched out like gum and whipped away before she could quite hear herself speak, as if the air around them were bending.

Shadows and sun gained speed.

Night. Stars overhead, turning like a wheel.

Light. Dark. Light. Dark. Light. Darklightdarklightdark-lightdarklight . . .

I might throw up, said Moo.

Amy gave her a hard look and said, "Well, DON'T."

Sleep took them. Or dizziness. It all seemed very much the same.

12. DID THAT JUST HAPPEN?

WAKING UP.

Waking up was a bit of a disappointment.

Everything was the same.

Everything except the chair itself, which had fallen over on its side. And the clock, whose face had cracked. Cameos and kettles and baby teeth and most of the rest of the contraption had come unstuck and lay scattered along the edge of the pond.

Moo and Amy had landed on opposite sides of this mess.

Amy lay somewhat uphill and awoke looking up through leaves and branches, into dim sunlight and clouds. Searching about, she discovered Moo down by the water. Indeed, with her feet *in* the water.

Immediately Amy reached for her head and felt her hair, her face, her ears, and everything. *Am I all bloody and gross? Am I dying? Am I dead?*

She was none of those things. There was no blood. Her heart was still beating. She checked.

Okay. Well, good.

Moo, on the other hand, lay sprawled out and unmoving. Possibly dead. Amy got up and went and stood over her and poked her with the toe of her shoe.

Don't, said Moo.

"I was waking you up."

I've been awake.

Amy helped Moo to her feet. Helped her swipe twigs and damp leaves from her hair and clothes.

Nothing's changed, Moo remarked, sighing. *It all looks the same.*

"It does NOT all look the same. There's no witch. There's no . . . no US smashing out of nowhere and crashing and bleeding and . . . and so it's very different, you see. *What just happened?*"

Amy was surprised to find herself crying and shaking. She tried to stop and couldn't.

Okay, said Moo. *Fine. It's not the same.*

"How can you be so calm about it?"

I'm not calm. I'm catatonic. Inside I'm blubbering and peeing all over myself.

"There was a witch," said Amy. "How could there really be an actual witch? Was I seeing things?"

Why was she surprised? Her parents had *told* her there was a witch. She had more or less believed the story, but a story and an event that's really happening are two very different things.

You weren't hallucinating, said Moo. *I saw it, too. All of it. Now let's go.*

"Go?"

Yes, please. Since there really is a witch, apparently, I would like to not be here, in the woods. Obviously, we're somewhere else in time, but it might be five minutes or five hours away, and since we don't know, I think we should leave.

The idea of doing something, going somewhere, helped Amy calm down. She stopped shaking. She linked arms with Moo and led her away through the wreckage of the clock chair.

"If the chair is all cracked up," she wondered aloud, "then how come my head isn't bloody, and . . . what does it mean? What did we see? What happ—"

We don't know, said Moo, interrupting. *Until we do know, can we not panic about it?*

This either made a great deal of sense, Amy thought, or no sense at all. She decided to go with it.

And they walked and walked, and sniffled every now and then, and mostly didn't panic. Mostly.

WE STILL DON'T KNOW the way out of the woods, said Moo.

"Yeah. But we know which way it's not."

Amy guided Moo, as gently as possible, past the mossy rock and the fallen tree, until the woods thinned out and opened up, and there was the pasture. Cow-free, at the moment. The cows often wandered.

The girls crossed the field and climbed the fence, looked both ways before crossing the road, and reached the porch, where they had started the night before.

Amy waited for the door to fly open and for Moo's mom to come exploding at them, all crying and mad and happy and sad and relieved and going to kill them both. But this didn't happen. Not yet.

Will you take me into the house? asked Moo.

I was kinda planning on leaving you here on the porch, Amy thought, but didn't say. Moo heard her anyway.

Coward, she said.

"No way."

To prove it, she kept hold of Moo's hand and knocked on the screen door.

NOW it would happen. The screaming and exploding.

Crickets.

Just go in, instructed Moo.

So Amy pulled the door open, and in they went. Moo stiffened a little as they stepped over the threshold, but said nothing.

The inside of the house was pretty much what Amy had imagined. Sort of bare, sort of wooden and plain. A couple of pictures hanging on the wall. Stairs going upstairs. Off to one side, a room with a threadbare couch and a television.

Upstairs a toilet flushed. A door opened.

Footsteps.

Moo's mom appeared at the top of the stairs.

Amy squinted. Something wasn't right. Was her hair different? Had she gained weight?

Then she was distracted by Moo, who had begun tugging at her hand, gripping hard.

"What?" whispered Amy, facing her. "You're hurting my . . ."

She shut up when she got a look at Moo's eyes, which were dark and wild.

"What?"

That's not my mom! said Moo.

13. [SEVERAL WORDS UNSUITABLE FOR YOUNG PEOPLE]

"ARE YOU GIRLS LOST?" asked the woman.

That's not our couch, said Moo, sounding breathless, *or our TV, and the walls are the wrong color, and . . .*

They ran.

"Girls?" called the strange woman, behind them.

They ran around behind the house, over a tiny creek, past a high-voltage electrical station thingy—

"Over there!" gasped Amy, pointing.

To their right, up a shallow hill, stood a scraggly bunch

of trees. Not really a woods, just one of those places where trees grow simply because no one has thought to build anything there. The girls ran up the hill and hid themselves the best they could between a birch tree and a tree that looked like the letter W.

They grasped each other by the wrists, breathing hard.

It WORKED! said Moo finally. *The time travel thing!*

"It did!" wheezed Amy.

It worked a LOT! added Moo.

"I agree!"

Well, NOW what do we do? Who is that in my house? If we went through time—a LOT of time!—where are we? I mean, when?

Moo was in a tizzy. She flapped her arms like a bird, as if trying to figure out the unbelievable thing that might or might not have happened. Her eyes were wild, but also focused and bright. Before, her eyes had been so vague, so far away, and Amy realized—

"Moo," she said.

Moo froze. *What?*

"You're moving."

Huh?

"Moving. Your arms and legs and whole body! You ran all the way here from the house without me helping one tiny bit!"

Moo's eyes bugged. She gaped down in wonder at her

own legs, and her mouth cracked into a bright, wobbly smile.

"Just like you said would happen," said Amy. "Once you had more and more practice. Or once something scared the *mrrzzl* out of you bad enough. . . ."

Moo wasn't paying attention. She was busy waggling her fingers in front of her face.

Amy's mind whizzed like a blender. Things that weren't possible were happening, and a list of questions that she didn't have answers for had started burning in her brain. They went like this:

1. When are we?

2. What has happened to our parents, if they aren't where they're supposed to be?

3. Who's going to feed us and give us a place to sleep, et cetera?

4. Who was the witchy woman in the woods who tried to grab us?

It wasn't a long list, but it was important, and it was scary.

Amy said a word that was generally considered unsuitable for young people.

What? asked Moo, stopping in midtwirl.

Amy repeated the word.

I've never heard you say one of those words. My mom says them, but—

"It's an experiment. I'm scared almost to the point of losing consciousness, and I thought it might make me feel better."

Did it?

"A little."

Moo, too, said an unsuitable word.

"Well?" said Amy. "Better?"

Somewhat. How interesting. How useful. It's like a magic spell almost.

Amy thought of how her dad always said "mrrzzl" when she was around, instead of actually swearing. She wondered if this had the same effect.

"Mrrzzl," she said.

No. It did not seem to have the same—

What are you doing? asked Moo.

"Another experiment. See—"

Tell you what. While you're doing that, I will try to work on some of the actual problem-solving problems we are faced with at the moment. I have a list. Would you like to hear it?

"Of course."

Here's my list:

One: I have to go to the bathroom like you wouldn't be-lieve.

Two: We are both covered in dirt and guck from being in the woods, and sleeping on the ground, and messing with all that moldy, cobwebby old stuff.

Three: We should put our hoods down and look less like two kids with horns and antennae, and maybe draw less at-tention.

They put their hoods down.

Now the bathroom problem, said Moo.

"Easy enough," said Amy. They were surrounded by trees, after all. All they had to do was find, maybe, a tree with some bushes around it, and—

A sudden fluttering of wings interrupted her, and a large black bird landed on a fallen branch before them.

Both girls squeaked and then looked the bird over. A curious sort of bird, with a long, considerable beak and a feathery poof atop its head. It returned their gaze, seem-ingly unafraid, with sharp, orange-rimmed eyes.

"Okay," said Amy. "Weird!"

The bird cocked its head, as if listening.

"Okay, weird!" it said loudly and clearly. "Let's solve the bathroom problem first."

14. THE POSSIBLE WITCH

*H*OLY COW! CRIED MOO.

Both girls hopped back a step, mouths hanging open.

"It's like a parrot," said Amy.

Or a cockatiel or something! added Moo.

Astonishment quickly turned to amusement. Amy said an unsuitable word, hoping the bird would repeat it.

Before the bird had a chance, however, another voice spoke up.

"He's been taught to mind his manners," said the voice, directly behind them. "And he's neither a parrot nor a cockatiel. He's a Mutitjulu hearsay bird. Quite rare!"

The girls whipped around and discovered a tall figure in a long, dark coat (or was it a cape?). She wore a hood, and a hat with a wide brim, casting her face in shadow. A wicker basket hung from one arm. She carried a walking stick in the opposite hand.

Witch! thought Amy, thought Moo. They both struggled not to pee their pants.

The hearsay bird flapped over the girls' heads and perched atop the stranger's walking stick.

Possibly a witch, anyhow, thought Amy. Was it the same witch from before, from the big woods?

It can't be! thought Moo.

Indeed, this person looked much younger. Unless they'd come back in time a lot further than—

They should run. Both girls thought this but couldn't quite get started.

Is there more than one? said Amy to Moo. *Is this place practically overrun with witches, and no one's ever really noticed?*

"Where I come from," said the Possible Witch, "one replies when spoken to. If one doesn't wish to be considered rude."

"Rude!" repeated the hearsay bird. (A bright, winged

face hovered like an emoji over the bird's head. Its expression seemed to shift and change constantly.)

Amy and Moo exchanged a look. "Hello," said Amy in a voice that almost didn't shake.

The Possible Witch took a step toward them. A surprisingly long step, so that she began to loom over them somewhat. Amy looked for some sign, some floaty magical thing that would give them a clue about this person, but there was only something dim and ghostly over her head, like a cloud that hadn't decided yet whether it was going to rain.

"We're not really supposed to talk to strangers," she told the woman, taking a step back. "It's nothing personal."

"It's a fine rule," said the Possible Witch. "A rule I endorse. But I couldn't help noticing that both of you seem somewhat lost. My own mother raised me to be helpful, you see, and . . . yes, indeed, there is a certain far-from-home quality about you. Something I can't quite put my finger on."

The woman reached out suddenly and lay a long, stick-thin finger alongside Amy's cheek. Instinctively, Amy gave a small cry and stumbled back.

A tendril of luminous green stretched between her face and the woman's finger. It pulsed once. Then, as Amy retreated, it snapped in a shower of sparks that swam and faded like fireflies.

The Possible Witch straightened up, examining her hand and saying "My!" in a tone of surprise and wonder.

The hearsay bird, too, looked surprised and repeated Amy's unsuitable word.

Seeing that the stranger was distracted, Amy and Moo whirled and bolted.

Out of the woods, into some weeds, around a mud puddle.

Faster, faster, faster! they said to each other.

Amy kept expecting to hear the Possible Witch right behind them, reaching for them, moving fast on long legs, stretching out with long arms.

She glanced over her shoulder.

Instantly she wished she hadn't, because the witch *was* there! OMG, she really *was*, with the hearsay bird rising into the air above her, and her long, bony fingers reaching toward them.

"Oh, girls!" she was calling. "Girls, now, really!"

"Don't look!" Amy shrieked in Moo's ear. *"Go, go, gogogogogogogogogogo!"*

15. OFFICER BYRD

MOO GRABBED AT AMY'S elbow.

Police! she shouted.

Amy shook her head, tugging at Moo's wrist. "We can't go to the police!" she said. "They'll ask questions! Questions we don't have answers to, and—"

No! cried Moo, pulling at her, slowing down. *Police! Look!*

She pointed insistently, and Amy calmed down enough to see where she was pointing.

Ahead of them, visible between two brick houses, a cop cruiser sat at the end of a long suburban street, pausing at a stop sign.

Without a thought, the girls ran between the houses and dove behind a shrub.

One way or the other, thought Amy, *we've had it. Either the police or the Possible Witch . . .*

The Possible Witch, she saw, was still behind them but had stopped. The hearsay bird landed at her feet.

"French fries," it said.

The Possible Witch appeared to be watching the police car.

The cruiser left the stop sign behind and turned down the street toward them. Slowly, watchfully, the way cop cars do. Sort of protective-looking, but also kind of scary, even when you weren't wearing a stolen butterfly hoodie.

The Possible Witch backed up, turned, and walked away swiftly, back into the scraggly little woods, her bird waddling behind, chattering something indistinct.

"She's gone," said Amy.

Shhh! said Moo.

"What? The cops can't hear us; they're, like, a football field away."

They saw us. I know they did.

"They'd be driving faster if they'd seen us. And they'd

put on a siren or yell at us on the speaker not to move and stay where we are."

The cruiser advanced. Its headlights were like eyes, looking straight at them.

"She had that green stuff on her hand," Amy whispered. "Did you see it?"

Of course I saw it. We just traveled through time; how would we not have green stuff? Now shut up.

"But *she* saw it, *too*! Didn't you see her see it?"

I saw her see it! Please stop using your Loud Girl voice, please!

The cruiser was HUGE now. It crawled down the street right in front of the house and slowed down.

"Well, doesn't that surprise and disturb you?"

Not as much as the police disturb me at this particular time.

Maybe Moo had a point. The cruiser had pretty much come to a stop, and—

It sped up, turned down a side street, and was gone.

"Oh. Oh my God," said Amy. "Oh, good, good, good."

I agree, said Moo. *And I still have to go to the bathroom.*

Amy had to go, too, she suddenly remembered, and had to press her knees together to keep from you-know-what.

We need someplace to GO, said Moo in a strained voice, *and it isn't going to be in the woods. That leaves us with . . .*

It left them with the shrub they were hiding behind, they realized.

"I won't look at you if you don't look at me," said Amy.

Whatever, said Moo, and—

The scene where they pee behind the shrub does not need to be part of the story, don't you agree?

It is important to note that Amy finished first. Out she came, feeling much relieved, and walked—casually!—down to the sidewalk. It was a beautiful day, she noticed for the first time. Not only that, but she started to think the neighborhood had a familiar look and feel to it. This was probably her own actual neighborhood, she realized, although she'd never been down this particular street. Where was Cornish Road from here? She was busy wondering this and looking at the clouds in the nice blue sky, and didn't notice the police cruiser crawling back up the street until the officer inside rolled down his window and said, "Hi."

He might as well have said, "I WILL EAT YOUR SOUL!" Amy jumped a foot in the air and choked on an unsuitable word.

The officer raised one eyebrow.

"Is everything all right?" he asked.

The officer, Amy noted, had a symbol of a German shepherd floating in the air over his head.

"Yes," said Amy, very conscious that she was streaked

with dirt, that her hair was a tangled mess, and that she had peed on her left leg just the slightest bit. "Yes, I'm fine."

"What's your name?" asked the officer.

"Amy."

"Well, Amy, I have two questions. One: you don't LOOK fine. You look like a mudslide that came to life. And two: shouldn't you be in school?"

"Technically," Amy replied, "the first one isn't a question. It's a declarative sentence."

The officer raised his eyebrow again. "That's true," he said.

"What's *your* name?" she asked.

"A good, smart question," he said. "I'm Officer Douglas Byrd of the Troy Municipal Police. I'm the resource officer for the schools, in fact."

"Wow," said Amy, impressed.

"That means I'm the truant officer. Which brings me back to my second point. Why aren't you in school?"

Inside Amy's head, Moo's voice said, *Oh God! The cops! You're talking to the cops!*

I know! I'm sorry! He wants to know why we're not in school!

Tell him a dog chased us!

"A dog chased us," Amy repeated.

Officer Byrd looked up and down the sidewalk.

"There's no dog now," he said.

"I know. We escaped with our lives."

"Who's 'us'?"

"Huh?"

"You said, 'A dog chased us.' Is there a frog in your pocket?"

Moo emerged from the bushes and waved her hand.

"My friend Gertrude," said Amy. "The dog made us have to go to the bathroom."

"Gertrude," called Officer Byrd, "why don't you come on down here and be part of our conversation?"

Moo approached.

"She doesn't talk," Amy told the officer, tapping her head. "Head injury."

Officer Byrd looked concerned. "All right, kiddos," he said. "You're safe here. I'll make sure of it."

When he said this, a heart winked on like a light over his head, beside the German shepherd. Amy relaxed some.

She noticed for the first time that Officer Byrd's cop car looked kind of old-fashioned, with big, bulky lights—like gumball machines—on the roof.

"You guys go to Hook Elementary?" Officer Byrd asked.

"Yes," Amy answered. Well, good . . . her school existed in this time, whenever that was.

"Well, listen, both of you. Dog or no dog, I don't like

that you're wandering around on your own out here, when you ought to be in school. I guess you know a young man is missing."

Amy figured the smart answer was "Yes," so she said, "Yes." (Local people who weren't time travelers would be expected to know something like that.) (Also, her stomach jumped. She didn't like the idea of missing kids. No kid does.)

"He might even be in your class; you look about the same age."

Amy didn't know what to say to this. Her mind screamed like a jet, trying to think of something NORMAL-sounding to say.

Fortunately, Officer Byrd changed the subject.

"How about you two climb in, and I'll drive you on over to the school. They're bound to have some clean clothes you can change into. My niece tore her pants once, and the teacher had a pile of castoffs for her to wear. Hop in back."

Aw, man, Moo broadcast.

"It's an experiment," Amy chanted under her breath. "It's an experiment. . . ."

Yeah, said Moo. *You keep on telling yourself that.*

16. THE IMAGINARY, TERRIBLY BUSY, GRAVE-DIGGING MOM

IT SMELLED FUNNY IN the backseat of the cruiser.

Officer Byrd talked into the police radio, saying, "Twelve is ten seventy-six for Hook Elementary, heavy two young ladies."

The radio made a scratchy, squawky noise and said, "Ten four."

"Is that Spanish?" Amy asked Officer Byrd.

"Police Spanish." The officer laughed. "We talk in code to save time."

Police Spanish for "Take us to jail and trap us in the old-fashioned times," said Moo. *Plus, someone's going around grabbing kids. This feels less and less like an experiment.*

They were rolling down the street now. Outside the police car, neighborhood houses passed by.

They passed Amy's house. A strange, old-fashioned car sat in the driveway.

"What kind of dog was it?" asked Officer Byrd, glancing back.

Dang. Officer Byrd wanted details.

"It was a little dog," said Amy. "Like a Chihuahua, except with foofy hair. It wasn't big, but it was awfully mean."

Moo raised her eyebrows at Amy. She was impressed.

Officer Byrd nodded, and a minute later they pulled up in front of the school.

Hook Elementary looked the same, Amy was happy to see. A long, one-story brick building with windows like a hundred eyes. A wide concrete walk with a flagpole. A yard with some trees. Out in back, a vast green area opened up. Beyond that, some woods.

Of course, she still didn't know when they were, and she had no idea when the school had even been built. But the more familiar things looked, she thought, the better chance they had of not drawing attention to themselves. The better chance they had of getting back to the clock chair and back home.

You had to be super careful around adults. If they sensed you were up to something, they'd try to *help* you, and assume responsibility for you, and take over your life until they thought you were okay. If adults thought you needed help in a big way, they weren't very likely to let you just go on back to the woods and travel through time.

Officer Byrd let the girls out and walked them past the flagpole into the school.

The inside of the school, too, was unchanged and familiar: two halls, shaped like an L, with the library and office in the middle.

In the office (the same office), a secretary (not the same secretary) with dark hair sat behind a desk, wearing a set of glasses on a chain around her neck.

She put the glasses on and squinted at the three of them. And smiled.

"Hi, Doug. Nice to see you. What have we got? Runaways? My goodness, what did you do, bury them alive?"

"Dog attack, Mrs. Nyday," answered Officer Byrd. "Chihuahua."

"Terrible creatures." The secretary—Mrs. Nyday—addressed herself to the girls. "Were you bitten?"

Amy said, "No."

"I'm going to leave them in your capable hands," said Officer Byrd. He leaned down and looked Moo in the eye, and then Amy.

"Going to be all right?" he asked.

They both nodded. Amy added, "Thank you, Officer Byrd."

That seemed to be what he wanted to hear. He straightened up, said, "You're most welcome," and was gone, out the door and out of sight.

Leaving them to Mrs. Nyday.

"First things first," said the secretary, looking at them the way you might look at some dog poo that has presented itself at your desk. "Down the hall to the nurse's office with you, where you can wash, and I'll see if we can dig up something else for you to wear to finish out the day."

She led the way to a little medical-looking room and stood politely in the hall while the girls scrubbed at a tiny sink.

"Make sure you get under your nails," she called through the door. "Your nails are filthy. By the way, whose class are you in?"

Amy opened her mouth but got stuck. NOW what was she supposed to say?

I've got this, said Moo. *Tell her we're not in a class yet. Our mom was supposed to register us.*

Smart, Amy thought. And she repeated this little story for Mrs. Nyday.

"You're not registered?" asked Mrs. Nyday, leaning into

the room and frowning at them. "You're sisters?" she added, looking doubtful (looking SUSPICIOUS!).

We're both adopted, said Moo.

"We're adopted," said Amy, feeling like a parrot.

"Adopted? Well, that's always interesting. *I'm* adopted!"

Score!

"Still, I need your names, at least."

Amy told her the truth. Why not? "Amy Wood and Gertrude June Kopernikus," she said.

Mrs. Nyday frowned at Moo.

"Do you not have a voice of your own?" she asked.

Moo barked, *Tell her she's an insensitive old sourpuss who's going to get kicked in the knee if—*

"Actually, no," Amy told the secretary. "She had a brain injury, and now not being able to talk is her own personal individual challenge. Other than that, though, she's perfectly fine and, in her own way, surprisingly loud."

Mrs. Nyday looked apologetic. "Oh!" she said. "I was trying to be funny, and it wasn't funny at all. Anyway, your mother . . . ?"

Prompted by Moo, Amy said: "Mom was going to bring us in and get us registered this morning, but she got called in to work. She said for us to go ahead and walk to school, and she'd come in and register us later and everything."

The secretary was frowning again.

"Kids don't show up out of the blue, generally," she said.

"She called last week. To let you know we were coming."

"No," said Mrs. Nyday (now even her *voice* was frowning). "I would've made a note of it if anyone—"

"She said she didn't talk to the secretary. She talked to someone else who didn't usually answer the phone. But they took a message."

Mrs. Nyday was thinking; Amy could *feel* her thinking. It was like a pot of spaghetti cooking.

You're amazing, she told Moo. *You're like Mozart, except with a symphony of lies.*

Moo shrugged, saying, *I've been sitting on my porch unable to move or talk for a thousand hundred years. I sit and make stuff up. What else was I going to do? Tell her we're done cleaning up.*

"I think we're all scrubbed," Amy told Mrs. Nyday. "Necks and fingernails and knees and everything."

"Good girls," said the secretary. A minute passed while she rummaged in a closet and found some pants and a couple of gym shorts and socks.

"These'll get you through the day," she said, stepping into the hall while they changed. "I do wish we could get hold of your mother, to bring in some of your own things from home. Maybe we could go ahead and call her at work? I'd certainly feel better if—"

"There's no phone," said Amy, parroting Moo. "She doesn't work in a regular office place."

"And this irregular nonoffice workplace is where?"

"Out of town. I forget exactly where. We're still new. Everything's all so new. She's a professional gravedigger, at a cemetery, and there's no phone, out where the graves are."

"Well," said the secretary, "we'll need to stash you someplace for the day. What grade did you say—"

"Fifth grade, ma'am."

"Well, come on, then," said Mrs. Nyday, leading them out into the hall, past the library. "And don't 'ma'am' me. 'Ma'am' is for grandmas; I'm only forty."

Amy rolled her eyes mentally. Adults were always saying things like "I'm ONLY forty" or "ONLY twenty-two," as if they didn't know how totally OLD that was. People who were forty could have known Mulan or Andrew Jackson.

"What time is it?" she asked Mrs. Nyday.

"Just past one. You've missed lunch."

Waaay down the hall, stopping at—

Stopping at Amy's actual classroom door, the classroom she went to every day, back in the future. Wow!

"Hang on here a sec," said Mrs. Nyday, slipping inside. To talk with the teacher, Amy presumed. They would whisper together, and shrug and be irritated together. Adults were always irritated when unexpected things happened, or especially irresponsible things, like when gravediggers sent their kids to school caked in dirt, without properly registering, and one of them had brain challenges, and—

Mrs. Nyday was back. She shooed them through the door, saying, "You're all set, Amy Wood and Gertrude June Kopernikus. Have a good rest of the afternoon, and stop at the office before you go home."

"Okay," said Amy, and, "Thanks." She shut the door behind them and turned to face—

Amy's jaw dropped.

"Holy cats!" she blurted. "Mrs. BARCH!"

17. THE EMPTY DESK

IT WAS HER! NO doubt. But a different Mrs. Barch. This Mrs. Barch was a thousand years younger. She had dark hair and bright eyes and looked like she'd been ironed and made smooth.

My God, thought Amy, *how far back have we come?*

Besides Mrs. Barch, there were a bunch of schoolkids in the room. Half a million of them occupied their desks, all turned around in their seats, staring and judging, the way kids do. Thinking what all kids think when a new kid appears: *Is this kid higher or lower than me in the food chain? Will people like this kid better than they like me? Is the new kid friend material?*

"Hello and welcome," said Mrs. Barch (her voice wasn't scratchy; she sounded like what a glass of apple juice would sound like if it spoke to you). "We're partway through science, so just take a seat until we can get you sorted out."

A seat? Everything looked full.

"One of you can sit in the Cloud Chair," Mrs. Barch said, indicating one corner of the room. A wonderful reading corner, with a lamp and a bookshelf and a giant sock monkey sitting on a yellow beanbag chair, all arranged on a blood-red carpet.

Moo zoomed over and plopped down in the beanbag, propping the sock monkey up beside her.

The class made envious noises. Sitting in the Cloud Chair was a special privilege, apparently.

Mrs. Barch appeared to hesitate.

Then she pointed to the one empty desk, on the far side, in the second-to-last row, by the window.

"Over here for now, sweetie," she said, sounding uneasy. "Just till we get you organized and official."

Something was wrong. Only Amy and Moo could see it, but a shadow wound through the classroom like a dark spiderweb, touching all the kids, and Mrs. Barch, too.

"That's Oliver's desk," someone said.

Oliver?

The missing boy, said Moo. *Wanna bet?*

Oh no.

Amy stood beside the desk without sitting down, quite

A million eyes flared at her. She could hear the kid thinking, *Don't you dare. . . .*

She didn't look at the eyes. She looked out the window. Looked at the houses across the street. Leafy trees ros among the rooftops, the same trees she was used to see ing through these same windows, except smaller. A bird hopped across the school lawn.

"He's coming back," someone whispered in a shak voice.

Mrs. Barch had been holding a big *Teacher's Edition Earth Science* book. She now closed it and laid it down on her desk.

"I think so, too," she said quietly. Then, addressing Amy she said, "Amy, I'm sorry. How about you sit here at my desk today?"

Much better. She nodded eagerly, walked around be hind Mrs. Barch, and sat down in her rolling, swiveling, upholstered teacher chair.

Somewhere in the room, a couple of kids sniffled.

"Let's take a few minutes," Mrs. Barch told the class "to think about Oliver a little bit, and send him some good thoughts?"

Mrs. Barch, Amy thought, was a smart teacher. A teacher who knew there was no point in trying to teach science to a bunch of kids who were upset about something.

Mrs. Barch crossed her arms and looked at the floor. You could tell she was just as sad as the kids, but she was being teacherly and professional—

"He's *not* coming back," said a big, growling voice. "Why do you keep pretending like he's going to come home any second, when everyone *knows*—"

Amy zeroed in on the speaker, a big kid with hair like a mop. Hair that hid one eye, while the other eye—wow!—shone out like a blue torch. Like a spear. Like a tiny blue volcano. And he was dressed in a suit. A suit!

"That's ENOUGH, Henry," Mrs. Barch barked. "Everyone is very hopeful—"

"It's not hope!" Henry spat. "It's *denial*. My dad says so. Not only is he not coming back—"

"HENRY ZANE!" shouted Mrs. Barch, turning red.

"—she's probably EATING HIS HEAD right this very second."

Amy gasped. So did every other kid in the classroom. There was an increase in sniffles, and some actual crying began.

The witch! said Moo.

Amy swallowed hard.

Oliver's empty desk glowed like a big, sad candle.

A couple of other kids followed Henry Zane's lead. Two redheads—twins?—a boy and a girl wearing matching cowboy boots.

"She might as well sit in his desk," said the girl, pointing at Amy.

"She could even use his stuff," said the boy. "That way it would be like he hadn't been eaten in vain, because—"

"Stop it!" said someone.

A couple of someones. One row behind Oliver's desk, another boy and girl (not twin-looking) had stood up and were staring at Henry Zane.

A boy in a dinosaur T-shirt and a girl in a sparkly dress.

"Or what?" shot back Henry and the redheads. Henry stood up, but he had a cautious look about him. A nervous look, even.

There was more to this boy and girl, Amy sensed, than met the eye. You could see it in the way the other kids looked at them.

"Henry," said Mrs. Barch in a certain voice all teachers have. And she didn't say anything else. She just pointed at the door.

Very few kids, even the meanest ones, would keep messing with a teacher once she'd unpacked that voice. Behind that voice was the murky, mysterious soul of an adult bristling with wizardly, grown-up powers, and—

"No," said Henry Zane.

Every eye in the classroom bulged. Every eye looked at Henry Zane, then at Mrs. Barch, then at Henry Zane again, and back at Mrs. Barch, then baaaaaaaaaack at Henry Zane.

Mrs. Barch did not yell. If anything, she became eerily calm.

"Heather," she said, "will you please press the call button for the office?"

Over by the door, the smallest kid in the class, a little girl with shining black hair, slipped out of her desk and reached way up high to push a white button like a plastic Tylenol. Then she climbed back into her seat and rejoined the rest of the class in gaping at Henry Zane.

Silence.

Henry Zane glowered at his desk, brooding like a dark lord. The redheads in the cowboy boots did their best to look just like him, doing exactly as he did.

Dinosaur Boy and Sparkly Girl stood quietly. Calmly. They might have been thinking about peanut butter sandwiches, they looked so calm.

Amy! said Moo.

What?

Look at the board. The chalkboard.

Across the room, Moo was using her head to point at the chalkboard.

What? Why was Moo trying to distract her? Amy wanted to focus on whatever was going to happen with the bad kids and Mrs. Barch.

LOOK! urged Moo.

So Amy looked at the chalkboard. It had the usual school stuff on it. Some notes about photosynthesis. A flag. Some chalk and erasers.

The date, said Moo.

The date was written on the board. Amy scanned it twice. Three times. Meanwhile, the class and Mrs. Barch remained quiet.

The board said it was **THURSDAY, SEPTEMBER 21, 1989.**

Amy did some quick subtracting in her head.

Then she said, "Holy crap!" out loud.

Mrs. Barch and the other kids looked at her for a moment.

"Thirty years," said Amy absently. Her head spun.

Way to be subtle, said Moo. *Way to not draw attention to yourself and, I might add, myself.*

The speaker on the wall came to life, and Mrs. Nyday's voice said, "Office."

"Hi, office," said Mrs. Barch, sounding breezy, but in a sarcastic kind of way. "I have three children in my classroom who think they don't need to do what they're told. Please send the police."

The whole classroom took a sharp breath.

"How about the principal?" asked the office. "Will he do?"

"I suppose," said Mrs. Barch. "But I was hoping for the police; I really was."

The speaker went *POP* and went silent.

Thirty years, thought Amy. Three times as old as she was now.

Who was the president? Was there a terrible war going on, or people landing on the moon?

The classroom door opened, and a large man in a suit and glasses stuck most of his big self through the door. He looked like a mayor of some kind. An unhappy mayor. This, presumably, was the principal.

"Hello, Mr. MacAfferty," said Mrs. Barch.

"Good afternoon, Mrs. Barch," he said. He nodded around at the kids, saying, "Kids," and the kids all said, "Hi, Mr. MacAfferty," more or less in unison.

"Who . . . ?" asked Mr. MacAfferty.

"Take a wild guess," said Mrs. Barch dryly.

"I'd hate to guess wrong."

"Mr. Zane," said Mrs. Barch. "Naturally. And Mr. and Miss Rue."

Mr. MacAfferty invited these three to accompany him into the hall. The redheads left their seats and filed frowningly out of the room.

"Henry," said Mr. MacAfferty.

"I didn't do anything," murmured Henry, his one visible eye slowly burning.

Over by the door, the small girl with the shining black hair whispered, "Henry said the witch was eating Oliver's head."

Henry made an angry noise and glared over his shoulder.

"[Unsuitable word]," he growled, and the little girl cringed.

Mr. MacAfferty must have decided that was enough. He came the rest of the way through the door and, moving nimbly for a big man, strode between two rows of desks and took Henry Zane by the arm.

"You can get up and walk," he said, "or I can pick you up like a little baby right here in front of everybody. Which is it, Henry: the easy way or the hard way?"

Henry got to his feet, still murmuring, and shuffled balefully out of the room.

"I'm telling my dad," he was heard to say as he left. And Mr. MacAfferty was heard to reply, "Your dad knows right where to find me, Henry." He sounded tired when he said it.

The door closed.

Mrs. Barch looked tired, too.

She waved her hand at Dinosaur Boy and Sparkly Girl, saying, "Sit down, sit down. I know you mean well."

Sparkly and Dinosaur sat down.

"I'd like to apologize to our new friends," said Mrs. Barch, raising a hand to indicate Moo and Amy. Speaking directly to them, she said, "We've had some worrisome times lately. It hasn't been easy for any of us. We all handle it in different ways."

"I'm sorry about your friend," said Amy.

"He'll be back," insisted Shining Black Hair. (Heather, Mrs. Barch had called her.)

Remembering what her dad had said—some kids had disappeared, some kids had been eaten—Amy was pretty sure Oliver would *not* be back and that things were going to get worse.

Don't say anything! said Moo.

Amy was going to ask Moo if maybe they shouldn't try to warn people, but just then the speaker crackled and made a loud *BOOOOOOOOOOOOOOOOOOOP!* noise.

Mrs. Barch looked relieved. She rolled her eyes and said, "Hallelujah." Then, to the whole class, she said, "Recess. Don't bother lining up. Just go."

18. HENRY'S PROBABLY GOING TO BEAT YOU UP

AMY AND MOO JOINED the flood of fifth graders pouring through the double doors and huddled together at the edge of the wide, crowded playground.

Thirty years, they both thought together.

Then Amy said, "The witch."

I know.

"We can't just say nothing! My dad wasn't kidding when he told me about this stuff. It's not a story or a game, Moo."

I know. Moo appeared deep in thought.

"What?" asked Amy.

There's the history thing, said Moo. *We could mess up history.*

"It's called a paradox," said Amy. "I know. I don't care. If the future depends on us letting witches eat kids, maybe it's not much of a future. Besides . . ."

Amy stopped talking.

About twenty thousand kids were standing around listening to them.

"Hi," said some of the kids, and to these kids Amy said "Hi" back.

"What are you TALKING about?" asked the kids.

Tell them we're doing a puzzle together. Like a science thing or a story problem, except without the math.

Amy repeated this aloud. Instantly most of the kids' eyes glazed over. They wandered off to play kickball or step on bugs.

A few kids stayed to ask, "How come your hair is like that?"

Amy and Moo had straight hair, more or less. Moo's looked like a helmet. The kids of 1989 had big, curly, foofy hair. There was a girl with enormous, EXTRA-foofy hair, and another girl wearing huge green plastic earrings, and another girl with a black eye. There was a boy with an eye patch, and another boy wearing a Taco Bell T-shirt.

"We're trendsetters," Amy told them.

"Just so you know," said Enormous Foofy Hair, "Henry's probably going to beat you up. Both of you."

"I wouldn't be surprised," added Black Eye.

"Henry?" said Amy. "The kid in the suit? Isn't he busy getting expelled?"

The kids all shook their heads.

"They don't expel Henry," said Taco Bell. "His dad's on the school board."

"*Mrrzzl,*" said Amy. "Why would he want to beat me up?" (Amy had never been beaten up. She was hoping to avoid it.)

Enormous Foofy Hair shrugged. "Because you're new. And because you started the whole thing about Oliver. And possibly because you're wearing costumes."

"Started it HOW?" asked Amy, ignoring the costume remark.

"By walking in the room, basically," said Black Eye. "Anyway, even if they DO expel him, which they won't, his dad'll say it was the teacher's fault, and won't ground him or anything. Henry's dad thinks Henry is a miniature Henry's dad and he can do no wrong. He could squirt paint thinner in the principal's eye, and Henry's dad would say it was the principal's eye's fault."

"They're rich," said Taco Bell, as if that explained it all. "They've been rich for, like, ten generations."

Amy was about to say something else, but her super-senses told her that recess was about to end.

Boop, said Moo.

BOOOOOOOOOOOOOOOOOOOOOOOOOOOOOOP! went the official booper, and the playground emptied like a giant toilet flushing.

"OPEN YOUR SOCIAL STUDIES books," said Mrs. Barch.

We don't have social studies books, said Moo, over on the beanbag chair.

I don't really care, said Amy, who was feeling worn out. She felt like if everyone didn't leave her alone for a while, she was going to bite someone's face off.

Mrs. Barch was feeling worn out, too, you could tell. She told the class to go to page 60 and read about Mesopotamia.

A boy in baggy jeans raised his hand and said, "We already—"

"READ ABOUT MESOPOTAMIA!" snapped Mrs. Barch, and so they did.

She quietly brought a book to Amy and a book to Moo.

"Read about Mesopotamia," she whispered. She drifted over by the air-conditioning unit and stood gazing out the window.

And that's how school went for the rest of the day. They read or pretended to read. Amy learned about polytheism, in which people worshipped more than one god. For a while, she battled sleep, and her head bobbed up and down. She spent some time being nervous about being thirty years in the past.

What if they never made it back? The school secretary and Officer Byrd and other grown-ups would see to it that they were adopted or something, she was sure. This made her almost start crying.

What's the matter? asked Moo.

Nothing.

Lies! You're sad and upset, I can feel it.

Fine. What if we never get back?

We will. We just need another old clock. I think.

Amy caught herself rolling her eyes and throwing her hands up in the air. Enormous Foofy Hair saw her doing this and gave her a weird look.

Sure! she thought. *Easy! Do YOU know where to find a replacement antique clock before grown-ups find out we're two kids running around with no parents and no home? Do YOU know how to get an antique clock with no money?*

Moo did a mental version of clearing her throat, and Amy looked up to discover Mrs. Barch standing over her, looking peevish.

"You're not reading about Mesopotamia," she rasped.

19. SOME KIDS TASTE BETTER THAN OTHER KIDS

At PRECISELY THREE O'CLOCK, the booper went *BOOOOOOOOOOOOOOOOOOOOOP!* and school came to an end.

Amy and Moo had, by that time, planned a stealthy escape.

We can't let them corner us and get us in the office, Amy had pointed out. *They'll—*

I know, Moo had said. *They'll put us in THE SYSTEM.*

The trick, of course, was to get out of the classroom

and the school quickly, but without garnering suspicion or attention. Grown-ups were like animals in the wilderness; nothing captured their eye and triggered their reflexes faster than a running child.

Amy spent the last thirty minutes of the school day worrying that Mrs. Nyday was going to come to the door and ask to see them, and then take them down to the office and make them wait until their mother materialized.

But this did not happen.

The booper *boop*ed.

Amy and Moo crossed the room and stepped casually out the door.

"Bye, Amy," said Black Eye, zooming past in the hallway. "Bye, Gertrude!"

It was just like any other day when the last bell rang: a stream of kids like the Mississippi River, yammering and calling out, some running and being yelled at not to run.

"Bye, Gertrude!" hollered Enormous Foofy Hair, headed in the opposite direction. "Bye, Amy!"

"Bye!" Amy hollered back.

The Mississippi River surged, momentarily, down the hall in the direction of the office, bearing Amy and Moo with it.

"Don't stop," Amy whispered in Moo's ear. "No matter what!"

I know! answered Moo. *You think I'm stupid?*

The river turned the corner by the library and burst through the open doors, shouting, muttering, yelling, singing—

"Amy Wood! Gertrude Kopernikus!" called a voice just as the girls were about to reach freedom.

Amy looked behind them. She couldn't help it. There was Mrs. Nyday, naturally, holding a clipboard, waving a pencil in the air.

Go, gogogogogogogo! hissed Moo. *Keep going, keep going, goinggoinggoing!*

But then they stopped.

Why? Because of something they saw. Both of them, at the exact same time.

Beyond the broad sidewalk at the front of the school, across the street, standing beside an old maple tree, stood the tall stranger from the woods. The Possible Witch.

She was looking right at them where they stood in the open door. Still wearing her big hat and hood. The hearsay bird squatted at her feet, probing the earth with its long beak.

As the girls watched, gripping each other's hands, the stranger waved a long, willowy hand at them.

"Girls!" they heard her call. "Oh, girls!"

Her fingers traced shadows in the air.

Amy and Moo said the same exact unsuitable word in a hoarse, terrified whisper and plunged back inside the school.

They managed, somehow, to swim against the irresistible current of kids. It was as if superpowers kicked in and carried them along, past a flustered Mrs. Nyday, and pelted them up the hall the way they'd come. Past the library again, past Mrs. Barch's room—

"Slow down there, Indy Five Hundred," said Mrs. Barch, leaning in her doorway. Her voice had kind of an automatic sound to it.

"Girls!" the secretary called after them. "GIRLS!"

Light speed!

Outside again, onto the playground with a hundred other kids all around them, and onto the grass beyond.

The school receded behind them.

Outside, the flood of schoolkids quickly spread out and dissolved in various directions, trickling off into the neighborhood, down sidewalks, across the grass. . . .

Amy and Moo kept running, straight into the woods on the far side of the playground.

Trees and weeds and underbrush surrounded them and enclosed them.

They stopped, catching their breath, leaning against a pair of elm trees.

"This sucks," said Amy. "They're going to look for us. They'll send the cops."

Moo nodded, breathing heavily. *We can make ourselves hard to find, though,* she said. *They can't look everywhere.*

"Yes, they can, practically!" Amy argued. "They can do a robocall to, like, everyone in the neighborhood, and send out texts and et cetera, and have everybody keeping an eye out. It won't be just cops looking, it'll be everyone, everywhere!"

You're forgetting something.

"What?"

It's 1989. It's old-fashioned times. They don't have robocalls and text messages. I don't know if they even have TV.

Hope!

"'Kay," said Amy. "But that's just part of the problem. Why was she waiting for us?"

Who?

"Don't play dumb just because you're scared to talk about it. The woman with the hat. The one who touched my face and saw the green stuff. Maybe the same, you know, *person* we saw back in the big woods, just before we took off in the chair."

Moo covered her face. She obviously didn't want to talk about it.

There's no such things as witches, she said. *Not in real life.*

"Yeah, well, there's also no such thing as going back in time, or being able to see spirits in macaroni and cheese."

Maybe she was trying to help us, said Moo, sounding uncertain.

Amy kept trying to think scientifically, looking for logical explanations for everything that was happening.

The other Possible Witch, said Moo, *is thirty years from now.*

Amy steadied herself.

"It's a mystery," she said. "A scientific mystery. For now maybe it just has to keep on being a mystery. In the meantime, we'll be careful. We'll be alert, and—"

Someone screamed.

Off through the woods, not far away. A kid, screaming. Amy and Moo both jumped a little and looked at each other.

There were several different kinds of screams in the Kid World. Amy had categorized them once, when she was bored at her grandmother's house. The categories were like this:

1. The way kids scream when they are having fun or when they get an excellent present or something.

2. The way kids scream when something scares them.

3. The way kids scream when they are having a frustrated meltdown.

4. The way kids scream when they are hurt.

"Number four," said Amy.

Huh?

"Never mind!" And they both ran through the trees, going where the scream was. Like all kids, they were curious. If something horrible or exciting was happening, they didn't want to miss it.

Another scream. This one came in the form of a word.

"STOP!" said the scream, in the voice of a little girl.

Amy and Moo jogged up a tiny hill, and the source of the screaming became visible.

It was the small girl from Mrs. Barch's class. The girl with shining black hair. (*Heather,* thought Amy.)

Heather was getting beaten up by an adult.

No, wait. It *looked* like an adult at first glance. It wore a suit and tie, and was big, but it wasn't an adult, it was Henry Zane. And not just Henry Zane; the redheaded boy and girl were with him.

Henry Zane had Heather in some kind of wrestling move, with her arm twisted up behind her. As Amy and Moo watched, he gave her arm a sharp yank.

Heather screamed the way you would scream if a fire started in your stomach.

The redheaded boy gave her a kick in the knee.

Heather kicked him back somehow. He looked surprised.

"Say you're sorry!" Henry Zane was growling in her ear.

"Say 'I'm sorry I pushed the button to call the office and got you suspended, Henry!'"

Henry Zane looked REALLY mad. His hair was all wild, and flipped back so you could see both eyes. Both eyes were like ice caves, but also like knives.

"I'm SORRY!" cried Heather in a choking voice.

"SusPENDED!" snarled Henry Zane. "I don't GET suspended, you [a whole string of unsuitable words that would turn you into a salamander if you actually heard them out loud]!"

Heather sobbed. She was crying so hard she was drooling.

"I'm feeding you to the witch," said Henry Zane matter-of-factly. "I don't know why I didn't think of it before. Some kids taste better than other kids, you know. I'd probably taste sour, but I bet you'd taste pretty good. Mmmmmmm-mmm!"

Heather would have screamed again, except Henry Zane smashed a big hand over her mouth.

"All I have to do is tie you to a tree and leave you," he added.

"LET HER GO!" Amy shouted.

Amy hadn't really known she was going to shout. It surprised her. She remembered that one of her goals in life was to NOT get beaten up by Henry Zane.

But you were supposed to stand up for people. She knew that. She had been taught that in school, and by her parents.

Mostly, though, it just made her so MAD, seeing Henry Zane doing what he was doing. Heather was less than HALF his size, plus he had two people helping him.

While Amy was thinking these thoughts, Moo stomped down the hill and gave Henry Zane a powerful, angry shove.

Wow! She caught him by surprise! He fell back and landed on his butt with a huge **THUMP!** and made a hurt face.

Moo, Amy noticed, had her hood up and appeared to be glaring at Henry Zane with enormous plastic cow eyes.

Heather, suddenly released, stumbled off to one side, grabbing at her arm.

The redheads looked surprised. Their mouths hung open. They looked momentarily brain damaged.

Holy cow! thought Amy, running down to stand beside Moo (raising her hood as she went, feeling her antennae bend and bounce). *That was the bravest thing I ever saw in my whole entire life.* (Why wasn't *she* that brave? There were probably soldiers in the marines who weren't that brave.)

Moo started to answer, but just then Henry Zane's eyes went supernova, and he scrambled up off the ground, big dirty hands grabbing for Moo's throat.

Amy squinched her eyes shut, stepped right in front of Moo, and got ready to hit Henry Zane SO HARD right in the . . .

Except Amy didn't have the first idea how to hit anything. Henry Zane just sort of ran into her and tripped over her, and they all went down sprawling in the dirt.

Amy opened her eyes just in time to see the redheads running away.

And also to see Henry Zane jumping up again, cursing so hard it didn't even sound like a language at all, but more like he was trying to go to the bathroom with his mouth, and getting ready to jump on Moo and land on her stomach with both feet.

Amy had time to think that this was going to hurt Moo really, really badly. Raw fear knifed straight down through her whole body, and she felt sick.

Which was when a couple of voices screamed, **"NO, HENRY!"**

The voices were kid voices, but they were big, too, somehow. They were the voice version of Moo's mighty shove.

On top of the little hill stood the brave boy and girl from class, the ones who had stood up to Henry Zane. They looked mad. They had also changed clothes. The dinosaur shirt and the sparkly dress were gone, replaced with matching T-shirts.

Her shirt said KUNG. His shirt said FOO.

Really? thought Amy. Who *were* these kids? The original anti-bullies? The original frickin' superheroes? Did they actually *know* kung fu or—

Henry Zane stopped getting ready to jump on Moo's stomach. He curled his lip, bared his teeth, and said, "This is none of your business."

Kung and Foo struck very convincing ninja poses.

Henry Zane looked like he wanted to run uphill and punch the two of them in the face, but he also looked uneasy.

"Your turn's coming," he growled at Kung and Foo, and his raging eyes looked like they were having dreams about where he was going to kick them and twist them, but for now he seemed to decide that he was outnumbered.

He didn't run. He just walked away, looking strange and out of place in his suit, with twigs and leaves all over him.

"Thanks," Amy said to the boy and girl on the hill, getting up off the ground, brushing dirt from her borrowed clothes.

But the superheroes were gone.

She galloped up the hill in time to see them walking off together through the trees.

Hmmmm.

Okay.

Moo climbed the hill and stood beside her.

That's when Amy heard a low, terrible-sounding growl. The hair stood up on her arms.

Moo looked embarrassed. She grasped her stomach with both hands and said, *Shhhhh!*

"Oh, wow," said Amy.

Her stomach started growling, too.

If we don't find something to eat, said Moo, *we're going to digest our own bodies from the inside out.*

Amy shook her head and said, "How do you even *think* of something like that?"

20. OUTLAWS

THEY DECIDED TO STEAL some food.

Seriously, what else were they going to do? If they knocked on someone's door and asked to be given dinner, chances were that they would *get* dinner. And get the police called, plus social workers. A whole army of responsible grown-ups would come rampaging in and scoop them up.

They couldn't *buy* dinner. They had no money. Amy wasn't even sure if they used the same money anyway, back thirty years ago. They probably still used gold coins or polished stones.

So before leaving the woods, Amy and Moo decided that they would go to the grocery store and smuggle some food out.

"You're an expert lie teller," Amy told Moo. "Well, I'm an expert shoplifter."

You shoplifted a hoodie, said Moo. *One time.*

"But I did it expertly. I used diversion tactics."

Moo looked impressed.

Fine, she said. *Lead the way, Miss Expert Person.*

Off they went to get dinner.

THIRTY YEARS IN THE future, Amy was used to shopping at a grocery store called Kroger.

Kroger was like a city. It was a supermarket on one end, and all through the rest of the store they had everything else. Garden hoses. Gum. School supplies. Headphones.

Kroger was not too far away. Down one street, across a soccer field, down another street, and then across a giant parking lot with a Walgreens, a Big Boy restaurant, and a vitamin store.

Amy knew how to get there, but just to be safe, the girls tried to walk on streets that were sort of out of the way, keeping an eye peeled for the Possible Witch. Amy kept expecting her to drop down out of a tree, or come whizzing down the street on a bicycle, but she didn't.

It took about twenty minutes to get there. Long enough for Amy's stomach to actually start hurting, she was so hungry.

Then, when they got to the big shopping area, it was different.

It was still a shopping area, but the Walgreens wasn't a Walgreens. It was called Harper Drug, with an old-fashioned sign. The Big Boy restaurant was a place called the Empire.

And no Kroger.

Instead of the great big city-store, there was a much smaller, old-time grocery called Pangles.

Pangles didn't look like the kind of place where you could buy garden hoses or phones or vacuum cleaners or hats. It looked like you could buy food there, and that was about it.

They went inside (casually, like all good thieves) and disappeared down the dairy aisle.

"Cheese and crackers," said Amy. "It's best to keep it simple, if you're going to shoplift stuff."

Whatever. We can get shampoo, for all I care, as long as it's the kind you can eat.

They found the cheese. Just like thirty years from now, they had packages of cheese slices, so Moo picked up one of those—

"No," said Amy. "It's bulky. We need something we can slip into a waistband or in our pocket."

She picked up a package of Colby cheese shaped like a domino.

"We need to go down an aisle where you can't see the big, round mirror," she said.

Pangles had a couple of big, round mirrors, hung up by the ceiling, over *here,* and over *there.*

So they walked super casually down the aisle with the orange juice and apple juice, and Amy stuffed the cheese into her pocket.

How nice of the school to lend them pants with big pockets! Was that a 1989 thing? Big pockets? A lot of the pants in the future didn't even *have* pockets. So much for progress. It was a wonder that people in the future could shoplift at all.

Crackers. Crackers were more difficult.

They stood in the cracker aisle, looking at the boxes.

A woman with a toddler in her cart went wheeling by. Down at the end of the aisle, an old man stood poking at loaves of Wonder bread.

The whole time they'd been in the store—about five

minutes—Amy hadn't seen a manager. This was a bad thing. Her one experiment in crime had taught her that it was good to know where the managers were. She had a plan, and it depended on finding a manager.

It also depended on the woman with the kid and the old man moving on to other parts of the store, which they soon did.

Open one of the boxes, Amy told Moo.

Okaaaaaaay . . . Moo acted like she was reading the back of a box of Ritz crackers and smoothly tore the box across the top.

Inside the box were four long packages, in wax paper.

So, said Moo, *now what?*

Amy told Moo the plan that had taken shape in her head, and Moo exclaimed, *I don't THINK so!*

Well, do you have any better ideas?

Moo didn't. And she was sooooooo hungry. Her stomach made a noise like a mastodon gargling mushroom soup.

Fine, she said, and stuffed a package of crackers into her waistband.

A MINUTE LATER, THE store manager—a tall, thin, slightly greasy-looking man with a name tag that said SCOTT—was carrying a twenty-four-roll package of toilet paper past the cash registers when a young girl with glasses and long, messy hair came blasting down the frozen pizza aisle and jumped up and down in front of him.

"There's a **RAT**!" she shrieked. "Oh my God, a big, huge RAT stuck in the freezer thingy back there! A RAT with RED EYES and—"

Scott went into full panic mode. His eyes popped, and he made desperate shushing motions at the girl. Then he sprinted down the pizza aisle, loudly whispering, "Where? Show me! Where?"

The girl trotted after him, saying, "Over there! Over there, I think! I *think* it was a rat. It might have been a possum. OMG! Possums are even worse! Yes, I'm SURE it was a possum!"

Customers followed Scott with their eyes, looking disgusted. No one noticed another girl, with curious eyes and bulging pockets, walking out the front door as casual as could be.

Scott came to a stop in front of the freezers, looking this way and that.

"I don't see it!" he said. "Point out where it was! Point . . ."

The girl with the wild hair was gone, probably frightened out of her mind.

Wouldn't *you* be, if you had seen a possum among the pizzas? I sure would.

AMY FAST-WALKED ACROSS THE parking lot, past the restaurant and the Harper Drug, and waited for Moo on the
far side of a busy street, in front of a church with a green
steeple.

Moo was laughing, Amy could tell, the whole way across
the lot. She was still laughing by the time she arrived at the
church.

She looked at Amy and said, *Possum!*

Amy laughed, too.

Did you see him? The manager? He's scarred for life, I bet.

"Well, I hope not."

*Well, me too, but still. Where are we going? I'm going to
eat this church if I don't get some food. I'm THIS CLOSE to
being like a pure animal.*

"The woods by the school," said Amy, who had thought
this through.

That's FIVE HOURS AWAY!

"It's not. Calm down. It's maybe—stop that!"

Moo kept reaching for the cheese, which was threaten-
ing to fall out of Amy's pocket.

"It's maybe twenty minutes. But we have to get out of
sight. Then we can sit down and eat in peace, and think
what to do next."

Fine, said Moo, but she said it darkly.

And they started walking. Away from the shopping center, back through the neighborhood. All around them, they could feel people sitting down to normal family dinners. Meat loaf. Macaroni and cheese. Salmon casserole. Spaghetti. Italian sausage and green peppers. Pork chops.

Amy found herself thinking about her mom and dad, naturally. At first, thinking about home made her smile a little bit. But the smile quickly vanished, replaced by a cloud of worry (an actual cloud).

What's wrong? asked Moo, who, of course, could see the cloud.

"We have to get back," said Amy.

Back to the woods? asked Moo.

"Back home."

Well, sure.

"No!" Amy said urgently. Her cloud darkened. "Nothing's for sure! The chair and the clock and everything are in pieces, and we don't know how we're going to fix any of it. If we make the wrong move, we'll get scooped up by helpful people and sent somewhere. Plus, we still don't know what that tall woman was all about."

But, said Moo, *we do know we're going to get home. We saw ourselves get home.*

"Oh yeah! Bloody and unconscious! You're not helping. In fact, that's a big fat reminder that things at home, in the future, are just as dangerous as—"

Dangerous?

Amy's cloud began to rain. "Something bad's going to happen!" she said, stopping in the middle of the sidewalk. "Back home, back where—I mean, *when* we came from. I don't know what, but *something*. I can feel it. Plus, that strange man who talked to Mom and Dad said it was really unlikely that everything would be okay. I don't even know what I can *do* about any of it, but maybe something, because we can see things and do things, you know? I don't know for sure about any of it, except I know we have to get back! We *have* to, Moo!"

She was crying now. Her shoulders shook. The little cloud turned black.

Moo stepped up and put her arms around her and squeezed.

Didn't say anything. Just squeezed.

Which was nice.

After a minute, Amy stopped shaking. She didn't feel better, necessarily. Everything that was wrong was still wrong. But she felt stronger, and that helped.

"I thought you weren't a hugger," she said, sniffling.

I'm not, said Moo, letting go. *But you are sometimes.*

Moo, thought Amy, knew how to be a friend.

Thanks, said Moo. Looking around, she added, *We should keep moving.*

Amy nodded. Then she stooped to pick up a couple of

pebbles. Handing one to Moo, she said, "More fuel. We need all the help we can get."

I never, said Moo, *heard anything more true in my life.*

They added the stones to the collection in their hoodie pockets and walked the rest of the way in silence.

In the woods, they found a nice spot where the sun shone down and was warm, and there were soft, dry leaves all around, almost like a carpet. Two gray boulders cropped up out of the earth and made nice places to sit. Some birds fluttered around and sang now and then.

Amy thought they were going to have a rough time getting the cheese open, but she must have underestimated how hungry Moo was.

Gimme that, Moo said, and bit one whole corner off, plastic and all. Amy wasn't sure if she actually chewed and swallowed the plastic, and she didn't ask.

They broke the cheese into blobs with their fingers the best they could, and made little cheese sandwiches. The sandwiches had little spirit-clouds around them. Like buttery halos.

The woods, too, like all woods, Amy supposed, were crowded with spirit-forms and meanings. The trees had parts of the earth and sky running through them . . . water and soil and nutritious nature stuff. The rocks were like bubbles from down underneath, where the planet was hot and boiling.

There was a soft breeze, with the soul of a grazing horse.

I have to figure something out, said Moo. (Her voice, in Amy's head, had a faraway quality that Amy recognized as meaning that Moo's thoughts were someplace else. It was a voice Amy recognized from her own thoughts. It was something the two of them had in common: they both often went places inside their own heads.)

"Figure out what?" asked Amy.

Moo took a deep breath. *How to talk to my mom,* she said. *It's gone on too long, all this silence. Her blaming herself for everything. Until we learn how to hear each other, nothing will ever change or get better.*

She sounded so sad. It made Amy sad, too.

"We can both think about it," she said. "It'll be sort of a thought experiment."

Moo nodded. She didn't say anything else.

But the breeze was an evening breeze, the kind that kicks up when the day world changes places with the night world.

It's going to get cold, said Moo.

Amy nodded. Man, she missed her house. Or even the camp in the middle of the field. She missed so many things she didn't normally have to worry about, like what she was going to eat, and what to say to people so they didn't put you in a foster home, and how to stay clean, and where to pee so she didn't get arrested. And how she was going to get through the night without freezing.

A blanket was a simple thing until you wanted one and probably couldn't get one.

They needed friends.

Amy wished they had done a better job of making friends that day during school. Of course, it was hard to know who to trust when you had only a couple of hours—

Before she could think about that very much, something bad happened.

21.
SOMETHING BAD HAPPENS

I T HAPPENED FAST.

Something slammed into Amy and was squashing her from both sides and pinning her arms down.

She started to yell but didn't get much yelling done before a couple of hands covered her mouth. At the same exact time, she saw Henry Zane loom up out of nowhere and wrap one big arm around Moo. With his other hand, he wrapped duct tape around her.

It was the two nasty punk redheaded kids who had her arms pinned, Amy realized.

"ARE YOU KIDDING ME?" she roared, except she didn't roar, because they had her mouth all covered.

She managed to bite one of them. HARD.

The kid shrieked and jumped away, hopping up and down, holding his hand between his knees. Then he got mad and was hopping back and looked like he was going to hit her, but suddenly Henry Zane was there, pushing him away. Pushed the other kid away, too, and *ZIP-ZOP* . . . an instant later, Amy was wrapped in duct tape.

ZOOP! Duct tape over her mouth, too.

Amy and Moo mentally exchanged unsuitable words.

"I'm sorry," said Henry Zane, "if you thought it was over earlier."

"I'm sorry, too," muttered Redhead Girl.

"I'm not," Redhead Boy muttered, and then coughed. He sounded like he might have a cold and wanted to go home.

Do you have any ideas? Amy asked Moo.

Yes, answered Moo. *Whenever you get a chance, kick them. All of them.*

There was a hard *THUD,* and Henry Zane gasped.

Moo had kicked Henry Zane right where it counted.

Amy lashed out, too, but only succeeded in rolling herself off her rock. She hit the ground hard and pain lanced her shoulder.

Man, she thought, *just last week everything was normal and great, and now I'm stuck in the 1980s getting beaten up in duct tape.*

The next couple of minutes were no fun at all.

Henry Zane and his redheads picked Amy and Moo up (despite a lot of kicking) and dragged them over to a pair of straight, strong-looking trees and duct-taped them to the trees.

They didn't just duct-tape them a little. They made mummies out of them. Amy worried that these angry, mean kids didn't know better than to wrap duct tape over their faces, and was in terror of getting smothered.

Moo might have been terrified of this, too. Mentally, she was a shouting, cursing, thrashing hurricane.

But their heads were left uncovered.

Henry Zane and his toadies stepped back.

"They're scared," said Redhead Girl.

Redhead Boy whispered that maybe it was okay to un-duct-tape them, now that they were scared, and Henry Zane slapped him on the back of the head.

I don't know what to do, said Moo.

I don't think we have choices, said Amy.

The duct tape made her feel claustrophobic. Something

panicky fluttered around in her head and chest. She struggled.

Nothing budged.

Henry Zane held something shiny in his hand now. He held it up so that Amy and Moo could see it clearly.

A knife! He was going to cut them free.

Or not. Oh God. Was he going to do something truly awful? Amy almost threw up. This was worse than being struck by lightning.

It was not a knife. It was a set of silver tubes dangling from a wooden disk, with strings. . . .

Wind chimes.

"Witches love these things," said Henry.

The breeze that had been blowing turned itself up and became an actual wind.

Henry tied the wind chimes to a medium-sized, low-hanging branch. As soon as he let go of them, they began to tinkle.

Tiny spirit-stars appeared and fell from them like snow.

That's what music looks like, Amy realized. *Excellent!*

If Henry Zane and all the other mean people in the world could see the things she and Moo saw, Amy wondered, would they still go around making other people miserable?

Because Henry Zane was complicated. Besides the Henry Zane she saw on the surface (the same Henry Zane everyone else saw), there was a spirit-Henry, and that spirit was a pair of eyes like the eyes of a dog. They hovered over his head and kept changing.

The eyes looked mean.

Then they looked afraid.

Then they looked mean again.

Then they looked like they wanted something, the way dogs look sometimes.

Then it became hard to tell the difference between these things.

The redheads, too, had spirit-signs. Two clouds. Clouds that changed shape constantly and were rainy-looking.

"That's all," said Henry Zane. "Let's go."

Amy realized that Henry Zane and the redheads were really going to leave them tied up to trees in the dark woods, and they really expected something to come and take them.

The bullies disappeared into the twilight.

The wind moaned through the trees.

The chimes rang softly, and then loudly, and then softly again.

THE NIGHTTIME WOODS ARE different from the daytime woods.

Different creatures come out. A lot of creatures hunt at night.

Like owls. Amy could feel them moving in the trees and whispering through the air.

Creatures scurried in the dry leaves.

The trees were different, too, and the rocks and moss and dry leaves on the ground. There were mysteries and unknown things, and buried time and buried memories.

The earth, like people, dreams at night. It's the time when the sun quits shining in your eyes and you can see all the way out into the universe.

Nightmares are a kind of dream. Amy certainly felt like she was in one.

There's not really a witch, said Moo. *Not that tall woman, or anyone else.*

Amy didn't reply to this.

There's not really a witch, Moo repeated.

Except I think there is, said Amy.

That's dumb, said Moo, sounding scared.

Well, said Amy, *do you want me to try and make you feel better, or tell you what I really think, so we can be realistic about things?*

MAKE ME FEEL BETTER! yelled Moo.

Silence for a moment. Just the chimes tinkling, dropping their musical stars and sparks and snow.

Moo said, *Okay. Being realistic about things is obviously the wiser choice. But is it really realistic, the witch thing? I mean, seriously?*

I've been trying to tell you, said Amy. *In OUR time, this is like something from local history. My mom and dad have told me about it. When they were young, like us, there was a witch, and she ate some kids. It's not like a scary Halloween story; it's an actual thing that happened. The witch actually got some kids.*

Oliver, said Moo.

And you and me.

Moo was crying now.

It's a strange thing to hear someone else crying inside your own head. It makes you feel like crying, too.

So they both cried.

And because they were two very exhausted girls, they soon cried themselves to sleep, where they shared fitful dreams and blurry mutterings.

22. MS. GOOLAGONG

AMY WOKE SUDDENLY.

It wasn't like one of those things where you wake up and don't know where you are. She was immediately sharp and alert, and remembered everything, and was just as scared as she had been before.

More scared, because something felt different now, and she didn't know what it was yet.

The wind had died down a lot, but it wasn't that.

The moon had come up, and the woods now had shapes and shadows made of dark and moonlight. Overhead the chimes stirred and sang. Musical stars fell.

Something, Amy knew, had awakened her, but she didn't know what.

Moo.

I'm awake, Moo answered. *I hear it, too.*

Hear what?

Branches creaked. An owl hooted.

There's something out there.

Amy wished Moo hadn't said that.

There are lots of noises, Amy said. *It could have been just about anything—*

But as soon as she spoke, Amy felt it. For the first time in her life, she knew what it felt like to know she was being watched. Just as surely as she knew when she was eating a ham sandwich or when her feet were touching the floor, she knew something was looking at her.

She watched the woods, barely breathing.

She found herself watching one particular part of the woods, actually. A tree half-hidden in shadow, half-bathed in moonlight. A tree with a peculiar, untreelike quality.

As Amy gazed fixedly at this tree, it moved, and was not a tree at all but a person.

Amy and Moo both screamed against their duct tape.

It was the tall woman.

Her silhouette was unmistakable: broad-brimmed hat, walking stick, basket, everything.

The Possible Witch was now Pretty Definitely a Witch.

The witch seemed to sense that she had been discovered. She took two long strides through dead leaves, making almost no sound at all, and stood right in front of the girls.

Amy's nose was running now, and she feared drowning. It seemed as if every system in her body had revolted. Terror hurt her stomach, her heart, her head. She felt like someone had installed a washing machine inside her. She thought she'd rather just die than feel this way much longer, and as she thought this horrid thought, the witch reached with spidery fingers for her face.

Amy closed her eyes and waited for her brain to be sucked out, or to feel the witch's teeth scraping against her skull.

She didn't feel these things.

She felt something fiddle with the duct tape on her cheek and then yank the tape off in one firm stroke.

OW! she thought.

Oh crap! thought Moo. *You're dead! I'm next! Are you dead?*

"Don't eat me," Amy said to the witch.

She couldn't really see the witch's face. Everything was

shadow or indistinct moonlight. Nevertheless, the witch inclined her head as if examining Amy and considering what she had said.

"Why not?" asked the witch. "Do you taste funny?"

OOoooh! What a witchy voice! It made Amy pee herself a little. The witch had some kind of accent, as if she had spent too much time saying spells or talking to the dead.

And then the witch had a knife! An evil, rusty, moonlit knife, and—

SLASH! SLASH! CUT! TEAR! *RIIIIIIIIIIIIIIIIIIIIIIII-IIIIIIP!*

Amy was free of her duct tape.

RIIIIIIIIIIIIIIIIIIIIIIIIIIIIIIIP!

Moo, too.

The girls stood rubbing their arms, adjusting their clothes, feeling sticky and gross (and wet) and confused (and smelly).

"Why not?" croaked a voice down on the ground. "Do you smell funny?"

The hearsay bird, a barely visible shadow in the moonlight.

"Tuba," it said. "French fries. The planet Mars."

Amy looked up at the witch—waaaay up—and said, "You're not a witch at all, really, are you?"

And the witch said, "Not even a little bit."

Amy felt ever so slightly disappointed.

"Not even a *little* bit?" she asked.

The tall, shadowy, moonlit person leaned down in a confidential way and whispered, "Perhaps one percent. But no more than that, surely."

And the tall, shadowy, moonlit person turned on her heel, secured her basket in the crook of one arm, dug into the earth and the leaves with her long, tapering walking stick, and went hiking away in the dark at great speed. The hearsay bird flew up and hitched a ride atop her hat.

"I think you'd better come with me," said the One Percent Witch, calling over her shoulder.

"With me," repeated the bird. "Fiddlesticks, we're out of coffee."

Both girls hurried after. In moments they caught up and were sailing through shadows in the mysterious woman's wake, between trees and around mossy rocks.

"Where are we going?" Amy asked.

"You're going with me."

"And who are you?" Amy thought she should ask. This moonlit person might not be a witch (a fact, Amy reflected, that they did not know for certain), but she *was* a stranger, and she *had* appeared in the woods at midnight, with a knife.

"I am Ms. Elaine Goolagong," said the One Percent Witch.

Goolagong? thought Amy.

"Is that an Irish name?" she asked.

"It's a name from a long, long time ago, and underneath the world," said Ms. Goolagong. "Which reminds me to introduce my excellent avian friend, a native Australian, who allows friends to call him Tuba."

"Tu-BA!" honked the bird. "TOOOOO-buh. TubaTUBA-tubatubaTUBAtubatubatuba."

"It's his favorite word," the witch explained. "Mine too, I think. Too-buh! Yes, quite."

Amy and Moo told Tuba that they were pleased to meet him, to which he replied, "Chicken strips." The emoji over his head split in two, grinning.

"He will," said Ms. Goolagong, "repeat anything, anything AT ALL, I'm sure you've noticed. He is fond of grocery lists and has a particular penchant for broadcasting anything you might consider private or sensitive."

Amy and Moo noted a tone of mild reproof.

Talking-bird issues, remarked Moo.

"That's what I get," muttered Tuba, "for buying cheap toilet paper."

"Hush!" hissed Ms. Goolagong, and they all marched on together.

THE WOODS GAVE WAY to grass, and then a sidewalk.

Ask her, said Moo to Amy, *if she's the same witch we saw thirty years from now, by the pond.*

Amy nodded. She had questions of her own. Like why had Ms. Goolagong been waiting for them outside the school, and how was she able to see the green time stuff, and did she know what it was? But it didn't seem like the right time yet for questions like these.

Not now, replied Amy. *Not yet. Besides, how would she even know?*

Instead she asked Ms. Goolagong, "Where are we going? In some detail? Please?"

"I am taking you home," said Ms. Goolagong. "I think if you follow—smartly, now!—and use your eyes and ears, you'll find your questions answered."

Amy and Moo traded startled glances. They *couldn't* be taken home, obviously. Not for thirty years.

"To *my* home," Ms. Goolagong explained.

They practically had to run to keep up with her. Did they have walking in the Olympics? Ms. Goolagong could win a gold medal! Tuba must have had practice; he rode her bobbing head like an old sailor on a stormy deck, bobbing and leaning when necessary, eyes straight ahead.

"Steady as she goes," he said.

Amy could hear Moo starting to pant.

"Ma'am?" said Amy. "Could we slow down just a small bit? My friend isn't really a running kind of person. She'd mention this herself, except she has a brain injury and doesn't talk."

I might just die, said Moo. *I might skip the barfing and just pass away completely.*

Ms. Goolagong slowed. Turning and walking backward, she said, "I'm very sorry. I forget that my legs are like two superpowers."

She walked backward with quite as much confidence as when she walked forward, as if she had eyes all around her head. Which, for all they knew, she did. Because they hadn't seen her face yet. There was the straw hat, with its wide brim, plus she wore a hood of some sort, plus it was dark, and even in the moonlight—

Then, suddenly, they DID see her face. Saw it quite clearly.

Because: FLASH! A set of headlights came beaming around the corner, and before you could say "Hsif!" (which is *fish* spelled backward), they spilled bright, sharp light all over the four of them. Especially Ms. Goolagong, who happened to be facing that way (and the hearsay bird, who squawked, "Mona Lisa!" and slapped an irritated wing over his eyes).

Ms. Goolagong, it turned out, was a queen.

She didn't have a crown on her head, but a girl knows a queen when she sees one. It wasn't just that Ms. Goolagong was pretty. She was pretty wrapped in midnight and stars. She was a full moon on a hot, misty night. She was a dusty sunset, with pyramids.

Space is said to be curved, and Ms. Goolagong's nose and neck were curved in the same elegant way. Waves of time and gravity are said to ripple through space, and Ms. Goolagong's loose blue gown rippled around her, touched by wind. Her hood was not a hood; it was her own hair, exquisitely braided, beaded and bejeweled like the rings of Saturn. The bird sitting on her head only lent her a certain mythical quality, as if she were, say, the goddess of the wild hunt.

Amy felt like bowing her head but could only gape as if her brain had been zapped.

Moo, crying, said, *That's what I want to be when I grow up. I love her!*

Amy was dumbstruck; she nodded agreement.

All of this took a mere second or two. Meanwhile, the car behind the headlights approached slowly and stopped.

Ms. Goolagong returned the glare of the headlights without blinking.

Amy and Moo did their best to shield their eyes and hide their faces.

They heard doors open.

"What are you doing with these girls?" demanded a voice (which was nervous but trying to be authorityish). It was the school principal, Mr. MacAfferty. "We've been looking for them, and so have the police."

"Amy and Gertrude!" called Mrs. Nyday's voice. "Come

over here at once!" (She, too, sounded nervous but bossy. You couldn't blame either of them, really. After all, there was a kid-eating witch in town.)

"Well," Ms. Goolagong muttered, "this kind of thing is why I tried to hurry us along."

Amy and Moo wobbled back and forth, not knowing what to do.

The witch's hands perched on their shoulders like great, wonderful birds.

"There's no need for a fuss," she said to Mr. MacAfferty and Mrs. Nyday. "These girls are my adopted daughters. I am going to make an educated guess that you are from the school?"

"You educated-guessed correctly," said Mr. MacAfferty. "But listen—"

"I'm afraid I owe you an apology," Ms. Goolagong continued. "I sent them off rather unprepared this morning. They tell me they may have been something of a bother."

"Well," said Mrs. Nyday, "we're happy to have them, of course. Nevertheless, there are procedures—"

"Procedures!" cried Tuba. "Equinox!"

"Yes, procedures," said Ms. Goolagong. "I hope that you will trust in me to register my butterfly, Amy McFoss Wood, and my lovely cow, Gertrude June Kopernikus, before they trouble you another day."

Whaaaaaat? said Amy. *How—*

Your middle name is McFoss?

It's a family name. Shut up, June.

How does she KNOW these things?

Shut up, that's how!

"I would have been on the spot this very morning," Ms. Goolagong was explaining, "if I had not been called to start early at my new job. I am the new chief sexton at Peaceful Hills Memorial Gardens, in Dayton, you see."

"The girls told us," said Mrs. Nyday, "that you were a gravedigger."

"A gravedigger and a sexton are the very same thing," answered Ms. Goolagong.

Amy couldn't help thinking that she had never seen anyone less likely to be a gravedigger than Ms. Elaine Goolagong.

"If you will excuse us," said the witch, "we are about a night hike, observing stars and insects."

"Pishposh!" said Tuba. "Out of clean underwear again."

Ms. Goolagong growled and gave her head a little jerk, provoking a peevish squawk.

"Actually . . . ," began Mr. MacAfferty.

But Ms. Goolagong had already turned and was striding away, her astonishing hands turning the girls, too, and pulling them along with gentle urgency.

The headlights swooped off down a side street, vanishing behind houses.

Amy was bursting with questions.

"How did you know—"

"My goodness!" exclaimed Ms. Goolagong to Amy. "On your head! A badger!"

Amy swatted at her head, found nothing. "What?" she said, confused.

Ms. Goolagong was suddenly quite serious and business-like. "We have confused the good people from the school with information," she said, "which is not at all the same as convincing them. The moment they can reach a phone, they will contact the police. I'm afraid our night hike in the open air must be at an end."

Was she leaving them? Oh no! Just when Amy thought they had found the friend they so needed!

She was opening her mouth to protest when Ms. Goolagong bent at the waist—bent waaaaay down—and lifted a manhole cover out of the street as if it were a five-cent coin.

"Down below," she commanded, pointing, straightening up. "There's nothing to follow up a night hike like a good old-fashioned tour of the sewers!"

23. FUGITIVES IN THE SEWER

THE GIRLS COULDN'T HELP obeying. Ms. Goolagong's voice was like that. If she told you that you were Yankee Doodle and that you must ride to Cincinnati on a purple wiener dog, you would believe her and you would do it.

They could complain, though, and they did.

"The sewers?" whined Amy, peering into the hole, making a face. A ladder ran down one side. At the bottom . . . well, she couldn't actually see the bottom.

But she did as Ms. Goolagong told her. Slowly, carefully, she knelt, lowered herself in, and started climbing down.

It smells! whined Moo, climbing in after.

"It smells!" Amy repeated aloud.

"It doesn't, actually," argued Ms. Goolagong. "Not like a bathroom sewer, anyhow. This is merely a storm drain. Now, be brave, and try and go a bit faster. There's a good girl."

"Good girl," repeated Tuba.

They descended.

There were ghosts in the sewer, Amy discovered. The sewer had a story, after all—memories of storms and rushing water.

As they climbed down out of the moonlight, it got dark.

And then there was light again. Up above, Ms. Goolagong wielded a flashlight.

It didn't take long to reach the bottom. Amy's foot splashed down (ew!) in something she hoped was water.

"Gross," she said.

Moo and Ms. Goolagong joined her moments later, and the witch aimed her flashlight down a tunnel.

"Now follow closely," she said, "and keep up."

Off she went down the tunnel (it was like being inside a giant toilet paper tube, Amy thought), bent over at the shoulders to keep from damaging her hat. Tuba had tucked himself into her basket, which he rode like a motorcycle sidecar.

"Mouthwash," he said. "Olive oil. Red wine and shoe-strings."

Great, Amy thought. Thirty years in the past, following a witch down a dark tunnel in the middle of the night, with a bird reciting grocery-list poetry.

"Ms. Goolagong?" she said.

"Yes, Amy Wood?"

"You said you were taking us to your house. . . ."

"And so I am. This sewer line ends very near my home."

How far have we gone? Moo wondered. *Are we still under your neighborhood, near the school? For all I know, we could be under my house.*

Amy shrugged. They had no way of knowing.

"Ms. Goolagong?" she said. "What kind of witchy things, exactly, can a one percent witch do? How do you get to be a *five* percent witch? Can witches turn people into hamsters, and do curses, and fly and—"

"I don't know, dear. I'm not that kind of witch."

What kind is she? asked Moo. (Amy couldn't help thinking, *Hopefully not the kid-eating kind.*)

"What kind are you?" asked Amy.

"The scientific kind."

"There are scientific witches?" (Moo poked her in the side and said, *WE'RE scientific witches, dork! Deep Science!* to which Amy replied, *Oh yeah.*)

"Growing up in New Orleans," said Ms. Goolagong, "I

did so well in my science classes that I received a scholarship to a famous university, where I studied with Professor Hayden Gasfellow. Perhaps you've heard of him. He discovered the Seahorse Galaxy."

"No," said Amy. "But maybe my parents have. They're scientists, and they know—"

"He also introduced me to my husband, Karora, and trained us to be radio astronomers. Radio astronomy, you see—"

"I know!" shouted Amy (producing a deafening sequence of echoes). "There's all kinds of energy washing around in space, getting sent out from stars and quasars and galaxies and things. Some of it is in a form we see with our eyes, which we call light, and then some of it is X-rays or infrared or radio waves. Scientists learn about space by keeping track of all of those things."

"Splendid!" crowed Ms. Goolagong (more deafening echoes).

"Superglue!" answered Tuba, adding to the din.

The witch sped up. They passed over something skeletal that might once have been a rat.

Amy paused to acquire two stones (pieces of discolored concrete, really). She offered one to Moo.

NO! protested Moo. *Nasty!*

So Amy kept both.

"Perhaps," said Ms. Goolagong, "in regard to Karora, it

would be best to backtrack somewhat. He began life not in a city or anything like it, but near Uluru, in the great Australian desert. Instead of television, his family had, for companionship, the moon and the sun and the stars. Imagine! With no cities nearby, no artificial light polluting the sky, Karora grew up under a night sky like infinity on fire! Stars by the billions! He took such an interest in outer space that his friends and family called him Avakasayatri, 'the astronaut.' They pooled money to send him to the university, to Professor Gasfellow."

"I think *I'd* like to study with Professor Gasfellow," said Amy.

"Well, you can't," said Ms. Goolagong. "He's quite dead. Choked on a pea. Anyhow, after graduation Karora and I built our little house in the woods, and an immense radio dish in a big, huge open field. During the day, we taught classes at the university. During the night, we listened for signals from other civilizations, far out in space. Our little house had a lot of computers and printers that made graphs, and oscilloscopes and fuzz-wahz and cyclometers and—"

"What are fuzz-wahz and xylom-whatevers?" Amy interrupted.

"Complicated machines that analyze and foozlize, vooglerize and spaghetticize," answered Ms. Goolagong. "We were very good at using these machines. Together, Karora and I discovered the Rose Galaxy, the Peanut Galaxy, galaxy NGC HG3784698, the Ouroboros Ring, and the Birthday Cake Nebula."

Holy cats, whispered Moo, impressed.

"Are you guys still married?" Amy asked. "Is he back at the house?"

"What an excellent, nosy question. Very scientific! The answer is quite sad, I'm afraid. Tuba, dear? Perhaps you would feel better tucking your head under your wing awhile. I'm going to talk about the thing you don't like to talk about."

Tuba buried his head in his feathers.

"How sad is it?" asked Amy.

"It's sadder than a broken teapot," answered Ms. Goolagong. "Sadder than someone playing a saxophone in the rain. One day, you see, Karora decided to send a message OUT into space, instead of just listening. Sort of a great, ten-thousand-watt, cosmic 'HELLO!' Tragically, lightning struck the vooglerizer just as he was sending, which caused him to broadcast himself into space as pure energy."

Amy's jaw dropped. *Wow,* she thought, *people don't know half the things lightning can do!*

Jerk! said Moo. *Say something sympathetic!*

"That's awful, Ms. Goolagong. I'm so sorry to hear it."

"That's kind of you, Amy Wood. It has been difficult. All I have left of him is Tuba, who Karora brought from Uluru as an egg. Some people have children; I have this rather inconvenient talking bird. Life is unpredictable."

They passed some mold that looked ready to reach out and grab them.

"I'm afraid," said the witch, "that I haven't been back to the university since then. Mostly, I poke around looking for wild strawberries and nuts and mushrooms. Besides—"

WHAM! Amy ran right into Ms. Goolagong's behind. The tall woman had come to a stop quite suddenly.

"Oof!" said Amy.

Ms. Goolagong held up one hand, spider fingers outspread, saying, "Hush now!"

She seemed to be listening. All Amy could see of her was a silhouette. Beyond her, the beam from the flashlight revealed dull concrete, darkened with wet splotches. Somewhere, water dripped.

What's wrong? asked Moo.

I don't know. Shhh.

Even Tuba seemed to understand and was silent.

And then she heard it. Heard what Ms. Goolagong had heard.

Voices.

Behind them. Faint, but echoing in an unmistakable voicelike way. And not just voices, but a scratchy, squawky, electronic sound that was familiar. Why was it familiar?

A police radio! Speaking Police Spanish!

"Ms. Goolagong—" Amy began, but before she could actually say anything, the witch did something surprising. She turned, reached back with her long, long arms, scooped up both girls, and carried them—lickety-split!—down the tunnel like a couple of footballs.

"My apologies, girls!" she (loudly) whispered. "This must seem very rude, but I think that all three of us would rather avoid being detained by the police."

Amy and Moo looked at each other around Ms. Goolagong's rear.

Why does she want to avoid being detained by the police? they both wondered.

Because she's been eating kids like popcorn! they couldn't help thinking.

Shut up, shut up, shutupshutup! they told each other.

Ms. Goolagong managed to shoot down the tunnel without scraping the girls against the walls very much, and also somehow kept hold of her long, tapering stick and her basket and her bird. The flashlight she had stuck between her teeth, and she kept it aimed straight ahead as if she had become the world's strangest choo-choo train.

Tuba poked his head up. "One advantage of living alone," he said, "a lady can pick her nose all she likes, and no one's the wiser."

"I'll bet you taste just like chicken," snapped Ms. Goolagong, and the bird vanished once again into his plumage.

Ms. Goolagong's feet *skoooooooooosh*ed like flying boats through a series of murky puddles.

Amy realized that she no longer heard the police radio. "We haven't actually done anything very wrong," she said to the witch. "*Have* we?"

Ms. Goolagong laughed. "Nevertheless," she said, "it has been necessary for all three of us to tell a number of lies."

That's true, said Moo.

"And the good people at the school, together with their friends the police, certainly suspect these lies of being lies and will wish to question us on the matter."

Amy and Moo both agreed. They relaxed a little. This reason for running from the police was much less disturbing than the kid-eating theory.

"If we were to be asked a lot of questions," the witch continued (she wasn't even out of breath!), "I imagine a couple of girls would have a great deal of difficulty explaining why they had no actual house that they lived in, and seemed, for all intents and purposes, to have fallen out of the sky."

Splashsplashsplashsplashsplashsplashsplashsplashsplash-splashsplashsplash!

Moo was alarmed again.

How does she KNOW we don't have actual houses and things? Have we TOLD her this? Noooooooooo, we have not.

"How do you know," Amy asked the witch, "the things you know that you have no way of knowing?"

"Well," said Ms. Goolagong, "that is an interesting question, isn't it? We shall have to discuss it sometime."

"I thought," said Amy, "we were discussing it now."

"Did you hear about the girl who asked too many questions all at once and turned into a question mark?"

"No," said both girls.

"Well, she did. Or a lobster. It was either a question mark or a lobster. Sometimes people turn into lobsters for no good reason at all."

Amy couldn't help laughing. "No, they *don't*!" she argued.

"That's right. They don't. Now shush. You're making me tired, and we still have seven furlongs to go."

Splashsplashsplash!

"What's a furlong?" asked Amy.

"That's it!" barked Ms. Goolagong. "You're a lobster. Now be silent. Lobsters are silent."

They were silent.

A YEAR WENT BY. Well, an hour, anyway. But it felt more like a year.

At last, Ms. Goolagong came to a halt, set the girls

down, and led them up a ladder into the big, starry world above. Tuba, glad to be under open sky once more, leaped from the basket and swooped around them in wide circles, crooning happily.

They emerged well beyond the neighborhood, on something like a country road, with trees on both sides.

Amy suddenly realized that the road and trees were familiar.

"This is the witch woods!" she cried. "This is just down the road from your house, Moo!"

Why, so it is! said Moo. *Of course, it won't actually BE my house for years and years and . . .*

As they talked, the darkness got deeper, because Ms. Goolagong, flashlight in hand, hadn't stopped for conversation. She was off among the trees already, a shadow among shadows.

"You may join me or not," she called, "just as you like."

They joined her. Tuba took up his accustomed perch on her hat.

They hadn't gone very far when Moo mentally whispered: *Amy!*

What?

We're going into the witch woods with the actual witch!

Amy said she was aware of this.

Well, I just thought someone should mention it.

Fine. You mentioned it. Do you have any better suggestions?

Moo said that she did not.

They stuck with Ms. Goolagong and took their chances.

After a time, Ms. Goolagong stopped and said, "Here we are."

Ahead of them, occupying a small clearing and a pool of moonlight, was a little cabin.

A *familiar* little cabin.

Amy was only slightly surprised to see that it was the same cabin she and Moo had explored in their own time. The cabin in which they had found the chair and the clock. Except that this cabin had walls that were straight and windows that were whole, and didn't have a tree wrapped around it.

The door wasn't locked. It opened without a creak, and their host ushered them in.

The interior had a warm, sweet smell, the way Thanksgiving dinner smells, fresh out of the oven.

These smells inhabited a darkness relieved only by a single shaft of filtered moonlight, glowing softly through the window. Ms. Goolagong lit a match and brought an old-fashioned lantern to life. A gentle butterscotch light filled the room.

Like its future self, the cabin was filled with odds and ends. The same odds and ends, in fact, that the girls had already seen. Kettles, clock, dolls, pictures, buttons, radio, Egyptian cat goddess. Here, of course, they weren't dusty or rusty or fallen down. One of the kettles seemed filled with something hot, in fact, and sat atop the stove breathing steam.

Had Ms. Goolagong left the burner on while she went roaming? Amy puzzled about this. That seemed unsafe, and unlike Ms. Goolagong, who seemed so practical, in her superhuman way. Unless someone else was here, which no one was.

A familiar-looking (if newer, shinier) birdcage hung from the ceiling, near the window. Tuba zoomed straight to it and perched contentedly inside. His emoji closed its eyes and hummed as if meditating.

"Now," said Ms. Goolagong, shutting the door and herding them toward a blanket-smothered couch, "I need for you girls to have a seat here and make ready for a surprise."

If she's going to eat us, Amy thought, *now would be the time.* Would it be a surprise? She decided it would be. She was coming to trust Ms. Goolagong, whether or not it was wise.

They sat.

They prepared to be surprised (however a person does that, exactly).

"You can come out now," said Ms. Goolagong. "It's quite safe."

And someone crawled out of the oven. Someone— some*thing?*—furry and not too clean.

Amy and Moo nearly ran, but Ms. Goolagong captured them with her two long, strong hands and said, "Steady, girls."

Wild-eyed, Amy and Moo evaluated the thing that had emerged from the oven and discerned that it was a boy. A rather thin boy, with hair like a haystack and the same look in his eyes that a rabbit has when it is trying to decide if you have seen it or not, and whether or not you are dangerous.

"Pancake batter," remarked the bird.

"This is Amy," said Ms. Goolagong to the boy, "and this is Gertrude. Girls, let me introduce—"

Oliver, said Moo.

"Oliver!" gasped Amy.

"Oliver," said Ms. Goolagong.

24. THE BOY WHO WAS EATEN

OLIVER DIDN'T SPEAK.

Not at first.

He simply advanced into the middle of the room and stood there looking around at shelves and the fireplace and the ceiling. Looking anywhere except at Amy and Moo.

Is he part ferret? asked Moo.

"Is he part ferret?" asked Amy.

Oliver made an offended noise.

"Don't be offended," Amy told him. "Moo is part cow,

mentally. I'm part lightning. It's okay to be made up of different recipes."

"I'm one hundred percent *person*," said Oliver, sounding tired. "I've just been hunting wild mushrooms most of today. I don't always look like this."

A glowing spirit-eye hovered over Oliver's head. It seemed to scan the room and the world as if it were on guard duty.

Why was he in the oven? asked Moo. *I don't like that he was in the oven. A kid-eating witch, if you think about it—*

"Why were you in the oven?" Amy asked the boy.

"Heard you coming," he answered. "Wasn't a hundred percent sure who it was. I HOPED it was Ms. Goolagong, but it sounded like more than just her."

Who's he afraid of? asked Moo. *It's too weird. He hides in the oven, HOPING the witch comes back?*

"Did you know everyone thinks you've been eaten?" Amy asked. "They do."

"Girls," said Ms. Goolagong, "give him some room. Perhaps Oliver would rather—"

"It's okay," Oliver interrupted. "It's good to talk about things. Secrets are bad for people, if you really think about it. Knowledge is like light. The more you see, the more you know. Yes, I know everyone thinks I've been eaten. The important thing is, I haven't."

Not yet, said Moo.

"Not *yet*," said Amy.

Oliver smiled at this and said, "That's right. Not yet."

There was a space just then, a silence, that was perfectly made for someone to hop in and suggest that everyone might be hungry, and that's exactly what happened. Ms. Goolagong bustled across the cabin, nudged Oliver into an armchair, and said, "I believe I'll put some noodles on."

This was followed by a pandemonium of pots and pans being clanged and banged and filled with water.

The moment their host said "noodles," Amy's mouth became a waterfall and her stomach said, "Pittsburgh!" (Which is what your stomach says when it's empty. Listen closely next time, and you'll see.)

Moo's stomach said, "Purple horse!" (which is the other thing stomachs say), and so did Oliver's.

"Purple horse," repeated Tuba. "Pittsburgh. Marshmallow Jell-O."

There was no talking while Ms. Goolagong cooked. At first this was because of the sheer noise the witch produced. The pots BANGED, wooden spoons KNOCKED, boxes THUMPED, water HISSED from the spigot. Then the children were quiet because the cabin was warm and they were tired, and all three fell into an exquisite, dreamless doze.

They awoke to an abrupt cry of "Noodles!"

Ms. Goolagong presented them each with a red, steaming bowl. The cabin had filled with a hurricane of smells, some wild and spicy, some sudden and sweet.

No one said a word at first. Then all three children just said, "OHHHhhhhhhhhh!" in a way that was like a rising wind, and then they were busy awhile, eating. Tuba received a bowl of his own and was quiet and happyish like everyone else.

"Good?" asked Ms. Goolagong. "You can thank Oliver, in part. They're flavored with the mushrooms he picked."

I thought mushrooms were poisonous, said Moo. *Some of them, anyway.*

Amy repeated this concern.

"Some *are* poisonous," said Oliver. "You have to know what to look for. There's this one kind of mushroom called a pondhouse. It looks like a cross between a mushroom and a sweater: red, yellow, and black stripes all around it. Then there's another mushroom called the deathwatch, which looks almost the same, except the red and yellow stripes touch. The pondhouse tastes like a cross between candy and smoke; there are pondhouse mushrooms in these noodles. The deathwatch mushroom also tastes like candy and smoke, but it paralyzes your lungs and you die."

Moo and Amy froze in midslurp.

"Oliver," Ms. Goolagong admonished.

"Well, it's true," he said.

"Did Ms. Goolagong teach you about this?" asked Amy. "About mushrooms?"

"I already knew," whispered Oliver, looking at the floor.

"You don't have to talk about it," Ms. Goolagong said to him.

"Talk about what?" asked Amy.

"I'd like to tell," said Oliver. "It's a happier story than 'Poor Oliver got eaten up by a witch.'"

"Oliver got eaten up by a witch!" crowed Tuba, stretching his wings. "Oliver got eaten—"

"That will DO," scolded Ms. Goolagong. Turning to Oliver, she nodded, saying, "Very well. You talk while I get dessert ready."

She turned again to the stove, only this time she seemed to make an effort not to bang things around.

Amy was just wondering, since the noodles had been so sweet and fabulous, what dessert was bound to taste like, when Oliver said, "I used to be a ghost."

Amy and Moo stared at him.

Had Ms. Goolagong raised this kid from the dead? You had to be 80 percent of a witch to do something like *that*, surely!

"Not a real ghost. It's just how I used to think of myself, because I was invisible."

Cool, said Moo.

"Not really invisible. My parents just didn't look at me, usually. I had the kind of parents who never really wanted kids. And don't look at me like that; I don't feel sorry for myself, so there's no reason you should. Here's the thing: if you don't get used to your parents paying attention to you, it's not like you miss it. Besides, I saw what they were like when they paid attention to each other, and they weren't very nice. One time I counted, and they told each other to 'shut up' eighty-four times in one night.

"They weren't usually paying attention to each other, either, though. They paid attention to the TV. I mean, that's the picture I have of them in my head. On the couch, in the middle of the trailer. They didn't blink or move, and they'd turn out all the rest of the lights and sit there with that weird TV flicker going on. They were like zombies. One time they sat there and sat still for so long, so completely, that my dad peed his pants because he forgot to get up and use the bathroom."

Moo said, *My mom's like that, a little bit.*

"That's what I mean," Oliver continued, "when I say I was a ghost. They didn't see me, or anything else. They forgot to do stuff like unlock the door and let me in. Or make dinner. Or breakfast. Or go shopping. I'm serious. They were, like, undead, just staring into TV space. Until someone came and got the TV, because of money. They didn't usually have jobs, so sometimes there were hassles like that."

"Were they on drugs?" asked Amy.

"Dur," said Oliver. "Normal people don't just spend their

lives sleeping with their eyes open. Anyway, that's the reason why I got good at finding mushrooms. And mulberries, and mint leaves, and walnuts. You have to crack walnuts open with a rock. Also, if you put a rock in your mouth and suck on it, you don't feel as hungry."

Speaking of hungry, something dessert-like began drifting around in the air. Something that was part peppermint and part tiger went crouching and snarling up Amy's nose.

Oh. My. God! she thought, struggling not to drool.

She felt bad, though, smelling dessert smells while Oliver talked about his parents not feeding him. Was he for real? Amy thought about what Moo had told her, about her father. Amy wondered how many other kids she knew with secret troubles at home.

Amy's thought-train stopped in its tracks. Did she know kids who looked like everyone else on the outside but had horror stories inside them? She thought of going to Pangles with Moo, stealing cheese and crackers. There must be kids, she realized, who faced that kind of problem every day. Kids who sat next to her in science class, maybe. Thinking about it made her stomach turn sour and her face grow hot. She felt the same kind of mad she had felt seeing Heather getting her arm twisted or seeing the Big Duke looming over her town and her parents. . . .

"Why didn't you say something to the cops?" she asked

Oliver. Actually, she kind of snapped at him, without meaning to, as if it were *him* she was mad at.

Oliver seemed to expect the question.

"Who knew what would happen then?" he said. "At least I *knew* what to do, with zombie parents. You go in the woods and find something to eat. The woods are like a grocery store. You keep a sleeping bag tucked under the propane tank, in case you get locked out at night. See? So I was doing all right."

Oliver's version of doing all right, Amy thought, and *her* version of doing all right were very different.

"And then things got better," said Oliver.

Oh! thought Amy. *Good!*

"One day . . . you know what a sinkhole is? Where there's, like, a huge cave or something growing just underground, and one day the ground caves in and everything just falls down into the earth? One day a sinkhole opened up under the trailer, and—"

"*O-LI-ver!*" snapped Ms. Goolagong.

"One day," said Oliver, "they fell asleep with their eyes open and didn't wake up."

He was quiet for a minute.

Amy almost got up to give him a big hug.

"I'm not a hugger," said Oliver.

Can he hear, like we can? Amy asked Moo.

Moo shook her head. *I can't hear him,* she said. *Maybe he just sorta picks up on things. Some people are like that.*

Oliver said, "I wasn't there when it happened. I came home from school, and when I got close, there was an ambulance and a cop car and another cop car, and they were taking my mom and dad out all covered up. Like you see on TV sometimes. So you probably think, 'Well, that would have been a good time to say something to the cops,' and I thought about it. But I wanted to think about it for a while and not decide anything right away. So I backed up and went off into the woods, and stayed there for a long time. I wandered farther than I ever had before, and after a while I realized I had a problem. See, you have to *cook* mushrooms. Before, I would take the good mushrooms, like the pondhouses, into the kitchen, and Mom and Dad didn't care if I used the stove to cook stuff, as long as I didn't ask them to do it. Well, it wasn't like I could do that now, right? Plus, it was getting colder, and I had left my sleeping bag under the propane tank, and thought if I went back for it . . . well, I thought they might be looking for me."

"They were," said Amy. "Plus, the kids in your class have a thing about people sitting in your desk."

Oliver seemed surprised.

"They do?" he said.

"Yep," said Amy. "And Mrs. Barch stares out the window like she's looking for you."

Oliver looked all big-eyed just then, as if he might cry.

"I'm not going to cry," he said, and he didn't. He looked as if he was probably an expert at not crying.

Amy wanted to DO something. *Mrrzzl!* It made her so mad, and it was so confusing, how you could have people with perfectly good hearts over their head who had no idea how to help people who needed help!

We should take him back to school, she thought at Moo.

What do you mean?

I don't know. They love him there, obviously, even if they didn't used to do a good job of showing it. Maybe now, if we take him—

Shhh! Hey! Loud Girl!

Don't call me that! Amy seethed.

Well, what are you thinking? Do you want someone to take US back to school?

No, but that's different.

Is it? How do you know? We're not the only ones with a complicated story. If you want to help, fine. But don't think you can just barge in and take over someone's life.

Amy clenched her fists really hard. Her whole self clenched, actually.

I kinda barged into YOUR life, she said.

But you didn't try and take charge, did you? All you did was show up and figure out how to be my friend.

Amy bit her lip. What Moo said made sense. It also made her want to cry.

I think, Moo concluded, *that Ms. Goolagong will know what to do. How to help him.*

Amy found that she agreed.

Oliver had paused to catch his breath. Now he took up his story again.

"So one day I was thinking that if I didn't find a solution to my food problem, I was going to be a ghost for real before long. And while I was thinking this, I came over a hill with a bunch of mushrooms in my pockets, and there was this house."

"It's a cabin," said Ms. Goolagong, without turning away from the stove.

"A cabin," said Oliver. "And I knocked on the door, and here I am."

Quiet.

"Here you are," sniffled Amy.

She jumped down off the couch and hugged Oliver whether he liked it or not. It was like hugging a pile of laundry (which is to say that it was like hugging something made of clothes, and it was kind of squeezable, but without much inside it, and it didn't hug back or say anything).

"Thanks," said Oliver stiffly. (Okay, so he *did* say something.)

Amy returned to her place on the sofa just as Ms. Goolagong turned around, balancing five red bowls in her long hands.

"Pondhouse Peppermint Paradise!" she announced. "Here, come and take them; my hands are full."

The children obeyed.

"Peppermint breath mints," said Tuba, accepting his bowl with a happy, spinning emoji. "Mouthwash. Q-tips. Deodorant. Foot powder."

Inside her bowl, Amy observed, was something like ice cream. It was pink and white and swirly, with little red and yellow stripes here and there, barely visible.

And chopsticks.

How did you eat ice cream with chopsticks?

Ms. Goolagong told Oliver to scootch over and joined him in the quilt-covered chair. Then she lifted her bowl to her lips and used the chopsticks to kind of shovel the ice cream into her mouth.

It wasn't neat or pretty. She got some on her gown.

Amy did the same, and—OW! It was hot!

"Careful," warned Ms. Goolagong. "It's hot. It's not ice cream at all. It's Pondhouse Peppermint Paradise."

They all emptied their bowls in silence.

"So," Amy couldn't help saying to Oliver when she had

finished, "they *are* looking for you. And a lot of people seem to seriously think you've been eaten by a witch. At some point, don't you have to . . . don't they have to come and get you, and you go live with—"

"A foster home," said Oliver.

"Yeah," said Amy.

"No," said Oliver.

Oh.

Ms. Goolagong cleared her throat and said, "Young Oliver and I have made other plans."

"Ms. G. looked in her crystal ball and saw that a foster home wouldn't work out too well," said Oliver.

Ms. Goolagong gave Oliver a look.

"Maybe," she said, "I hadn't planned on telling Amy and Gertrude about that."

"Yes, you had," said Oliver, sounding pretty sure of himself.

Amy raised her hand as if she were in school and said, "When you guys say a 'crystal ball,' you mean it like kind of a metaphor . . . ?"

But Oliver and Ms. Goolagong both seemed to cut their eyes sideways at the same shelf, where something like a bowling ball made of glass sat between a piggy bank and a pair of tennis shoes.

"Ah," said Amy. "Wow."

What did she see? asked Moo.

"What did you see?" asked Amy.

"Foster homes can be very good places," said Ms. Goo-lagong, "and they can be very *bad* places. In any case, *I* am Oliver's foster home."

"Exactly," said Oliver.

"Is that . . . legal?" asked Amy. "I mean, I'm not an expert, but don't you have to fill out papers, and go to court and get permission, and—"

"Look!" cried Ms. Goolagong, pointing at the ceiling. "A spider in red pajamas, reciting the Gettysburg Address!"

The children all looked and then felt silly.

"Any more questions?" asked Ms. Goolagong in a voice that suggested there shouldn't be any more questions.

Still, Moo asked, *can she look in the ball for us?*

She sounded meek. She sounded like she really, really, really, really, really wanted Ms. Goolagong to look in the ball.

Before Amy could relay the question, Ms. Goolagong said, "I've already looked."

But, said Moo, *she hasn't even touched the ball since we got here.*

"I can see it from here," said the witch. "And I may as well tell you, I can't discern much. In fact, I can discern only two things, neither of which makes much sense at all."

She rose from her chair, collected all the red bowls, and stacked them in the sink.

"What did you see?" asked Amy.

"Oliver," she said, "you'll have dishwashing duty this evening. Girls, when he's finished, you may dry."

She stepped aside and stood looking thoughtfully out the window, much like Mrs. Barch had done earlier.

"What did you see?" Amy repeated politely.

"A gigantic, awful machine," said the witch (who, considering the crystal ball, must have been 70 percent witch at least). "And cows. Lots and lots of cows."

A brief but very busy silence.

"I like cows," said Ms. Goolagong. "Tell me about the cows."

25. A PLAN TAKES FORM

"IT MAKES SENSE," AMY told Ms. Goolagong, "if you know the rest of the story."

"I also see a most peculiar rocking chair, and some people camping in the middle of a field, atop a giant red X."

"Wait a minute," said Amy, suspicious. "You saw all that in the crystal ball?"

"Certainly," answered Ms. Goolagong, looking amused.

"I don't think you did."

"Well!" said Ms. Goolagong. "Is that polite? After I have fed you and saved you from the school people and—"

I think, said Amy to Moo, *she has been in our heads all along. I think she's just like us. I think she saw that we were witchy, too, the very first time we met. And it's why she was able to see the green stuff, and—*

I think so, too, said Moo.

It took you long enough, said the witch, *to work that out.*

"Something is going on," said Oliver, still scrubbing. "I don't know what, but I want you to know that I'm aware of it."

Ms. Goolagong cleared her throat and said, "The girls were about to tell us a very strange story. Weren't you, girls? About rocking chairs and cowbells and lightning and things?"

Moo and Amy looked at each other.

"I am experiencing an overload of confusion," said Oliver.

"Confusion," repeated Tuba. Sure enough, his emoji looked confused.

"Fine," said Amy. And she told the story of all the things that had happened to them, past and future. She even included some history: the story of the wild, free cows, and the famous truck wreck that had made them wild and free. Also, she finally got around to telling about the legendary, kid-eating witch.

"You told me about that already," Ms. Goolagong gently informed her, "quite without meaning to. At least it doesn't appear that I was ever captured, as far as you know?"

Amy said she didn't think so. Her parents would have remembered and mentioned it.

"Of course," said Amy, "you are very much blamed for the eating of three entire children."

Ms. Goolagong's expression was difficult to read. She seemed offended but also philosophical and very much amused.

"Say on," she told Amy, and Amy continued her story.

Oliver's eyes widened when she described the Big Duke. When she told about how her parents meant to block the machine with their own bodies, he made a whistling noise and mumbled something about bravery.

It is brave, isn't it? Amy thought. It dawned on her that she hadn't really appreciated just how dangerous it was, what her parents were doing. She knew that standing up to the Big Duke and the mining people was honorable, smart, and bold. But it could get them hurt really badly, and the thought of that sent a stabbing feeling through her belly.

I have to be there, she thought. *It's important.* She didn't know how she knew this, but she knew it meant that she would have to be brave, too.

You are brave, said Moo. *Remember, in the woods, when Henry was being mean to that Heather girl?*

I suppose that's true, Amy replied. But was she brave enough?

"Amy Wood?" said Ms. Goolagong. "You were in the middle of a story, dear."

Amy shook her head clear and picked up where she'd left off.

Ms. Goolagong looked concerned when Amy told about the lightning, and briefly examined the Lichtenberg figures on her hands. There was a second moment, when she told about the clock and the glowing wisps of pure time, when Oliver dropped a spoon on the floor and turned around, eyes narrowed, and said he suspected them of making things up. To which Amy replied, "Not this time," and Ms. Goolagong said, "No, love, it's all quite real and true. I can tell." But for the most part, the story made its journey from beginning to end without interruption, and left them all with a lot to think about.

There was a lengthy silence, punctuated by the ticking clock.

Then Amy said quietly, "I can't be stuck here. I have to get back. The strange man with the sports car who came to visit me and Mom and Dad said I have to be there. For whatever reason, I think if I'm not there, they'll get hurt."

She let herself cry a single hot tear. Ms. Goolagong reached over and took her hand.

Okay, said Moo, *obviously, we have to go back where we*

came from, if we can. We live there. My mom's there. It's where we belong. But what about you?

She looked at Ms. Goolagong.

"You can't stay here now," said Amy. "They're going to come looking for you."

"We're *not* staying here," said Oliver. "Ms. Goolagong says we're going to the dreamtime."

Amy blinked. She asked if that was north of town.

"It's a concept from Karora's people," she explained. "It's like saying 'the beginning place.' Like starting over."

Where? asked Moo.

"We don't *know* where yet," answered the witch.

"Well, you're going soon," said Amy. "Right? I mean, they're not just going to come looking for *you,* they're looking for *us* now, too. Right now."

Moo said, *I hope the dreamtime or whatever is a place where people are nice to each other. All people.*

"What a fine world that would be," said Ms. Goolagong. "But speaking of worlds, I daresay we might have used this particular world up, what with lies planted like seeds all around us, and me already suspected of eating poor Oliver."

"I wonder what I'd taste like," Oliver wondered aloud. "Mushrooms, I imagine."

There was a particular kind of silence then. Not a long silence, necessarily, but important-feeling and full of the sound of people thinking thoughts and trying on ideas. Like all silences of this kind, it came to an end when someone spoke, and that someone was Ms. Goolagong.

"We will go across time in this contraption the girls have made," said Ms. Goolagong, "and take them home. Perhaps with all of us steering the ship, we will be able to get you back to the right time and the right place in the right pieces. And Oliver and I will be part of that world. It will be our starting-over place."

"Our dreamtime," said Oliver wistfully.

Amy loved this idea. They could be friends with Ms. Goolagong their whole entire lives!

Moo sensed her excitement and said she was excited, too. Ninety percent excited, anyhow, and 10 percent suspicious of the whole thing. Still, she was eager to make her way home. She made a happy noise and said, *The first thing I'm going to do is kiss all my cows right on their noses.*

"They can take their parking ticket," sang Tuba, "and shove it where the sun—"

"Well and good!" said Ms. Goolagong, snapping her fingers. "That's as close to a plan as we are likely to get, in our limited time. Are there any concerns or objections?"

It was better than anything she'd thought of herself, Amy thought.

"It's perfect," she said.

It's very smart, said Moo.

Tuba threw back his head, opened his great beak extra

wide, and crowed like a rooster until they all covered their ears in self-defense.

Not everyone was happy and optimistic, though, Amy saw. Oliver had an odd look on his face, as if he didn't know whether he was going to laugh or throw up. The eye above his head spun like a panicking disco ball.

"I can't quite make out," he said, "whether this is all real, or a dream, or maybe a cartoon of some kind."

Ms. Goolagong stepped across the cabin in one great stride and pulled Oliver to her.

"The universe," she said, "is not only stranger than we suppose, but stranger than we *can* suppose. A very smart person named John said something like that. What do you make of it?"

"What I make of it," answered Oliver, "is that the dreamtime is about to become much more than a metaphor. It is a real thing that is going to happen."

The spinning eye above his head lost its balance, fell over, and passed out.

26. TORCHES AND PITCHFORKS

MS. GOOLAGONG GRABBED HER hat and her odd, tapering walking stick and said, "No time like the present, as they say. Your chair is nearby, I take it?"

Near enough, said Moo. *And it's really* your *chair, you know.*

"Indeed," said the witch. "Very good."

Outside, the wind breathed softly, like horses half asleep.

Someone should point out, said Moo, *that we are forget-*

ting one little problem? It's broken! The clock chair. It's like the engine that drives the whole thing.

"Aw, *mrrzzl*," said Amy. "Double *mrrzzl*!"

Ms. Goolagong stroked her elegant chin and said, "Hmmmmmmmm."

In the corner, by the bed, Ms. Goolagong's clock ticked and tocked. Close by, her rocking chair sat as if waiting for someone to set it in motion.

Amy's heart raced. Her mouth fell open. She looked startled.

"We *have* a chair and a clock!" she gasped, pointing. "We have, in fact, the same exact *actual* chair and same actual clock! We can just take, with Ms. Goolagong's permission, I mean . . ."

Then her brain did some science, without even trying or meaning to, and her face clouded over. Disappointment rained in her head.

"No," she said. "It's not that easy."

Why not? asked Moo breathlessly. *We wouldn't have to fix anything. We could just—*

"Because," said Amy, "if we take the chair and clock, they won't be there in the future, when we need them."

Ms. Goolagong nodded. "Amy Wood," she said, "you're beginning to think like an expert time traveler."

Amy looked troubled and remarked that time travel was beginning to make her extremely nervous.

"Well," said Ms. Goolagong, her jaw set in a most determined sort of way, "we will just have to be very good at fixing things, at least for a while, won't we?"

Before anyone could argue, she was out the door.

So off they went, in an uneasy little parade, trying to feel confident and not succeeding very well, and getting a C minus in faking it.

THE POND WASN'T FAR, but the night was darker than before.

Ah! Some light! Ms. Goolagong's flashlight. Plus the moon, which still shone but was setting.

"I changed my mind," said Oliver. "I believe I would taste like pork."

Why pork? asked Moo.

"Why?" asked Amy.

"Pigs are the animals most like human beings. I read it somewhere."

"Wouldn't it be chimps or something?" asked Amy.

Ew, said Moo. *Who would eat a chimp?*

I didn't say you'd EAT one, Amy replied. *I said I thought they were closer to humans than pigs.*

"People in Jamestown ate other people," Ms. Goolagong interjected. "Remember your history? The English colony that had such a terrible time. They had what they called the Starving Time, and it got so bad, they dug up the dead."

(Well, wasn't THAT just exactly the kind of thing you'd expect a witch to throw into a conversation?)

Their feet crunched in the dry leaves.

An owl hooted.

"Okay," said Amy, "but they only did it because they absolutely *had* to, right? They didn't enjoy it, or eat more than absolutely necessary to stay alive?"

"Yes and no," Ms. Goolagong answered. "Yes, mostly, that's just what they did. But one fellow dug up his wife and prepared her like a holiday roast. He lit candles and dressed in his best."

I would taste like a cow, Moo announced.

"I'd taste like chicken," said Amy. "Fried chicken."

"What about you, Ms. G.?" asked Oliver.

"I don't have to guess," said Ms. Goolagong, guiding them up over a hilltop. "I know for certain. I would taste like cane sugar and lemon drops."

The pond came into view. Wind ruffled its waters, scattering moonlight.

"What do you mean," asked Oliver a little darkly, "you know for sure?"

"When I was very young," said the witch, "I was lost in the woods for two entire weeks and was forced to eat my foot."

"Your FOOT?" cried the children.

"Your FOOT?" cried Tuba.

"And then my other foot, and both legs, plus my torso, arms, and head. When I was rescued, there was nothing left but my nose."

"Your NOSE?" they cried.

"Just so. I dressed it in this gown and stuck a hat on it and have done my best ever since to make the most of things."

Then, "Ah!" she exclaimed as they neared the edge of the pond. "Here's something like a shipwreck, except consisting of odds and ends and parts of things, and wire."

She shone the flashlight around. Here was the chair, largely intact. Here was the ivory cameo, here was the part of the clock that was like a cabinet, and here was the part that was like a little machine. Here was some of this, some of that, scattered around.

"It doesn't *look* like a time machine," Oliver remarked.

"Well," said Amy, "who knows what a time machine is supposed to look like?"

"Well," he said, "it *does* have a clock on it."

"Fine," said Ms. Goolagong. "It's a clock machine. Whatever. Now, there's work to do; let's begin."

They began.

* * *

THE WORK WENT FASTER than you might think. For one thing, Ms. Goolagong's hands seemed to operate like miraculous engines, or like great birds from a planet where great birds knew how to wind things and fit things together and make things tight and shipshape.

How the girls had ever made something like a time-traveling chair without her was something Amy couldn't fathom. Now and then Ms. Goolagong would say, "Hold this!" or "Use this wire to tie this thing to that thing!" and they would do it, and do it smartly, and the work proceeded.

Tuba wandered around, probing the ground with his beak, pecking under leaves and things, now and then bringing them a button or a cowbell or a piece of wire.

"Hot sauce!" he sang out when he discovered the birdcage hidden in the underbrush, and he dragged it over . . . flutter, flutter, hippity-hop.

The witch lay on the ground like an auto mechanic, doing something that made the chair creak alarmingly.

"Hold the flashlight steady," she told Amy.

In the middle of all this science and magic and possibly a good deal of guesswork, Moo found time to grab a handful of stones and slip one into everyone's pocket.

Really? said Amy.

Every little bit helps.

At last Ms. Goolagong stood, shaking dirt and leaves from her clothes.

"Oliver," she said, "I think you'll want to sit on my lap, once I get situated, and the girls—"

"Someone's coming!" said Oliver suddenly.

Someone was. They all could hear it as soon as Oliver spoke. Beneath the moan of the wind in the branches, there was a muttering. Like the muttering of a lot of people standing in line or sitting in church. Or like the muttering of people looking for witches and runaway girls in the dark, and running into trees and tripping over things.

"Someone's coming indeed," said Ms. Goolagong.

Amy didn't like the way she said it.

Above the angry voices in the dark, Amy heard the fizz and squawk of Police Spanish.

"*Fzzzzzzz!* Adam two six, four sixty-seven, are you ten twenty-five five nine, blah, blah—"

"They're quicker than I expected," said Ms. Goolagong. "We'll need to move things along. Amy, dear heart, turn the clock hands to twelve. I'm assuming we don't know precisely what time you left?"

"You assume correctly."

"Twelve it is, then. Hurry."

For the first time in a while, Amy thought about what they had seen when the time machine first *whoosh*ed them away. In her mind's eye now, she saw the blurred green vision of their very own selves appearing. Her very own self, with blood in her hair, looking limp and maybe unconscious.

Nearby she sensed Moo thinking and remembering the same thing.

Shh, hissed Moo. *Not now.*

Amy understood. Just now they needed for the witch to be 100 percent undistracted. She forced herself to concentrate on wire and wood, wondering who was approaching through the trees. . . .

Above, on the hill, the muttering swelled, like a church with a lot more people in it, all of a sudden.

"It sounds like an army," said Amy.

"It's not just the police," said Oliver. "It sounds like . . . everybody."

"Focus, loves," said Ms. Goolagong.

Amy reached into the clock and turned hands. Green sparks hovered around her fingers.

Flashlights appeared on the hill, flickering among the trees. Flashing on the surface of the pond.

Not just flashlights. There was another kind of light—a wild, brighter light.

"Torches!" gasped Oliver.

"I suppose they're coming to burn my house down," said Ms. Goolagong. "Lovely."

Tuba hunkered in the leaves, watching the hillside, nervously muttering about the phone company.

Amy gulped and turned the hour hand to twelve. Green tendrils stroked her arm.

"Moo," said Ms. Goolagong. "Is your chair supposed to have some sort of bell? Something to get it moving?"

Moo was staring at the torches up on the hill.

"GERTRUDE!" barked Ms. Goolagong.

Moo shook herself the way a wet dog does. She looked at Ms. Goolagong and said, *A tiny bronze rabbit.*

"Please find it."

Oliver and the girls frantically searched among the leaves.

Up on the hill, the voices suddenly exploded.

"THERE SHE IS!" someone roared.

"THERE SHE IS!" echoed a dozen more voices. "She's got those poor kids with her!"

"They're under a spell!" someone shrieked.

The torchlight brightened as a mob of shadows poured down the hill.

Amy glimpsed spirits and symbols atop a hundred heads: hearts and smoke and shadows and fear.

She also saw firelight reflected on metal.

"Tools," she said. "They have shovels and pitchforks and hammers and yard clippers and things!"

"Weapons," said Oliver.

Amy's heart WHUMPed in her chest. She had to fight to keep from running.

The rabbit bell isn't here! cried Moo.

"Look with all of your senses," urged the witch. "It will look like a note of bright, clear music."

Torches and flashlights flooded around the pond on both sides.

SPLASH! *Splash,* SPLASH! *Splash, splash, splashsplash-* SPLASH! *Splash!* Shadows came stomping through the water. Unsuitable words filled the dark.

Ms. Goolagong turned away from the chair then. Turned to face the hundred torches and flashlights. In her hand, Amy saw, she held her long, tapering stick. Getting ready to jab and smack at them, Amy supposed, and felt more afraid than ever. How could Ms. Goolagong, amazing or not, ever hope to hold off a hundred—

But Ms. Goolagong didn't raise her stick to strike anyone. Instead she raised the narrow end to her lips.

And Amy heard the strangest thing EVER in the history of her life: a peculiar, otherworldly music.

It sounded like a bumblebee the size of a planet.

B U U u u z z z Z Z Z Z Z z z z z z z z Z Z Z Z Z - z u u u u u u u Z Z Z z z z z z z . . . The music had legs and wings and great old fingers and eyes like moons. It was a mist. If there was a God and he had a voice, Amy thought, THIS was what he would sound like.

Like outer space snoring.

Like the center of the earth waking up.

Like the sun and stars talking about what they were going to do this weekend.

Amy felt it vibrate through her skeleton.

The mob felt it, too, Amy could tell, the way birds and dogs can hear an earthquake coming.

They froze. All hundred of them.

"What . . . ?" a single someone said.

"What . . . ?" whispered Amy, wonderstruck.

"It's a didgeridoo," Oliver explained. "An instrument crafted by the original people of Australia. She played it for me a night or two ago, when we roasted marshmallows—"

It's a diversion! shouted Moo. *Keep looking for the stupid rabbit!*

They kept looking, tossing up leaves.

The bumblebee music *buuUUZZZZZZzzzzzzzz*ed and *huuuuUUMMMMMmmmm*ed and seemed to come from all over, from under rocks and out of the trees. It held the mob as if it were a giant, invisible fist.

"IT'S WITCHCRAFT!" someone screamed.

A rock flew through the air. It splashed harmlessly into the pond, but the spell—if that's what it was—was broken. The shadows and voices closed in again.

Found it! shouted Moo, brandishing the little rabbit bell.

"Excellent, dear," said the witch. "Would you mind twisting this wire around it, where the ears meet?"

She sat down in the chair as she spoke, gesturing with her long, wizardly arms.

"Smartly!" she said. "There's no time. The rest of you, in my lap, if you please."

Amy and Oliver obeyed.

"MY GOD!" someone screamed. "SHE'S EATING THEM! SHE TOOK A BITE OUT OF THE BOY JUST NOW, I SAW IT!"

(Other voices, a very few calmer voices, disagreed with this. Amy thought she discerned the voice of Officer Byrd. . . .)

If they catch us, thought Amy, *we'll never get home.*

"They wouldn't hurt us," said Oliver. "I mean, they think they're saving us." But he didn't sound sure.

Someone in the midst of the crowd bellowed, "OUCH, dang it!"

And someone else hollered, "OW!" and a third screamed, "Evil spirit!"

A dark, swooping shadow darted through the mob. Something that might have been a dark angel or a demon but wasn't. It was a Mutitjulu hearsay bird in full protective battle rage.

Zip! The shadow got hold of someone's hat. *Zoom!* The shadow pecked someone's ear. *Whoosh!* The shadow bit fingers and noses.

"*Peanut butter!*" screeched the bird. "*Dandruff shampoo! I dare anybody to try and explain to me why I ought to shave my armpits!*"

His emoji was a thousand emoji, a blazing rain.

Here and there, a few people broke and retreated. Others slapped at the bird. Garden tools raked the air.

"Tuba!" shouted Oliver. "Oh no! Oh, be careful! Tuba, come back!"

Tuba swooshed through the air and perched on Oliver's head.

"I hate commercials," he rumbled. "*Hate 'em!*"

A torch came spinning through the air. It landed in the dry leaves and instantly set the ground ablaze.

"STOP that!" called one of the reasonable voices.

"WE'RE OUTTA TIME!" bellowed one voice. Others joined in. "SHE'S DOING SOMETHING WITCHY TO THEM!"

Dry leaves burn fast. Fire licked at the rocking chair. Amy felt her rear grow warm.

There! said Moo, giving the wire and the bell one final twist.

"Hurry, hurryhurryhurryhurryhurryhurryhurryhurryhurry-hurryhurryhurryhurry!" chanted Amy.

The mob wasn't a mob now. It was individual people surging toward them in the strange, wild light. A burly man in a red T-shirt. A thin woman with big, round glasses. Two men with torches, wearing ball caps. A man with a pointy beard, wet and angry-looking.

Another torch came whirling at them.

Ms. Goolagong's arm shot out, snatching it from the air.

"SHE'S GOT A TORCH!" someone cried out, sounding terrified.

A rock thudded on the ground, sending burning leaves flying.

THUD! THUD! Thudthudthud! THUD! More rocks.

A few voices hollering, "STOP! Use your heads!" (Quickly drowned out.)

The mob had a single story, Amy saw. A single spirit-shadow. It rose over them with blind, raging eyes.

"Gertrude," said Ms. Goolagong, "give the bell a flick with your finger, please."

Moo flicked the bell. It rang out high and lovely, a one-note song.

Nothing happened.

The burly man was almost on them. He lifted a shovel as if it were an ax, aiming for Ms. Goolagong's head. Or Amy's head or Oliver's or Moo's . . . He wasn't really aiming, Amy could see. His eyes were animal eyes.

Hands grasped the back of the chair. Someone tugged at Amy's elbow. Burning leaves all around, flying up into the air. The burly man swung the shovel—

No . . . someone had grabbed the shovel. A couple of

someones, struggling with Burly Man. Two surprisingly small someones, which was odd. Did they look familiar, or was it just—

It was Kung and Foo, the brave girl and boy from the school.

It's those kids! cried Moo.

Amy nodded furiously. Wow!

It was hard to tell if the two wannabe superheroes actually knew kung fu or not. They were certainly trying hard. The girl—Kung—had a grip on the shovel and had been lifted free of the ground. The boy—Foo—had wrapped himself around Burly Man's knees and was trying, without success, to wrestle him off balance, but—

Wow! Success! Burly Man went down! *SPLASH!* In the pond! Kung threw his shovel in after him. *SPLASH!*

Oliver and Amy and Moo waved at the heroes, all trying to talk and yell at once.

Kung and Foo turned around and lunged for them! Grabbed for them!

"Grab my hands, Oliver!" shouted Kung.

"Jump!" bellowed Foo to Amy and Moo, pulling at their ankles. "We'll help you!"

Amy and Moo tried to tell their rescuers that they were just fine, thanks, and didn't need rescuing, but they all wound up hollering at once, and there was already so much noise, so much happening.

"Try the bell again," said Ms. Goolagong. "Perhaps it's slow getting started, like some cars can be." Her arms coiled around them like warm snakes made of iron.

But Foo now had hold of Moo's arm.

A bunch of feathers squeezed out of nowhere. A long, strong, magnificent beak came pecking through the air. Its aim was perfect.

Ding! sang the little bell.

Kung and Foo looked startled. They fell back.

"Nothing's happ—" Amy began.

A great green *WHOOSH* whooshed them up, and the hands and torches and noise and dark all fell away and vanished.

Cows! sang out Moo, eyes closed, totally focused.

Ms. Goolagong squeezed them all extra tight.

"Cows!" she shouted.

"Cows!" yelled Amy. (Why not?)

"Cows!" sang the wonderful, wonderful hearsay bird. "Cows, cows, cows, cows, cows!"

Green *WHOOSH* and weightlessness and dizziness . . .

"HOLY [unsuitable word]!" screamed Oliver. His voice whipped away on the WHOOSH, and sleep spun in on them and washed over them, and—

27. THE STORY OF THE COWS

SOMETHING TICKLED AMY'S NOSE.

She opened her eyes.

It was just a leaf.

She brushed the leaf away and sat up.

The clock machine wasn't in pieces this time. It lay nearby, as if catching its breath. Perhaps the clock had gotten slightly catawampus, but mostly, this time, they seemed to have arrived across the years without getting hit by some kind of space-time baseball bat.

"Oh," said a leaf pile just a few feet away. The leaf pile stirred, sat, and fell away, revealing Oliver. He looked about, blinking, asking, "Are we dead? I was almost sure we'd be dead. Are we?"

Amy said, "No."

More leaves rustled. Moo and Ms. Goolagong appeared, rubbing their eyes, just uphill.

"Nasal spray," called Tuba, way up high in a tree. He fluttered down and took a seat on Ms. Goolagong's knee.

"Well!" yawned Ms. Goolagong. "Wasn't that thrilling! I hope to do it again sometime. Is everybody in one piece?"

Everybody was.

Amy stood. She felt a peculiar focusing of her mind and her whole entire self, turning her toward home.

"I hate to be awfully rude," she said, "but I think I should start home. I want to keep my parents from melting like grilled cheese out of pure worry. Plus, I also have to be there with them when the Big Duke gets there, which could be practically any moment."

"Peace," said Ms. Goolagong. "Stick together. That way we can all be certain of getting out of the woods in the right direction."

They all walked uphill, holding hands.

Between trees and around stones.

The light, Amy thought, looked as it should. It had a seven o'clock look to it. Tired and reddish and on its way out for the night, but not gone yet. The air felt like seven o'clock air.

"Well!" said Ms. Goolagong suddenly. "Look at that!"

There, around the side of a leafy, overgrown hill, was her house.

"Wow," said Amy. "I thought for sure they'd burn it down!"

But the house stood more or less as they had left it.

"I'm not surprised, actually," said Ms. Goolagong. "Would anyone like to know why?"

They all agreed that they *would* like to know.

"Can you imagine what happened when we left? What they saw, and how it looked, and what they thought of it and said about it?"

They all thought and considered.

"A tall person in a wicked-looking hat grabbed you children up and vanished in a green flash! Right out from between their fingers, literally. Now, if that had happened to you, if those were your fingers, would you be in a hurry to go find that person's house and burn it down with your torches? Your silly torches?"

They all shook their heads.

I think, said Moo, *that I would be tempted to run out of the woods as fast as possible, and maybe never go in there again.*

Amy shared Moo's thoughts aloud, and Ms. Goolagong nodded.

"After a while," mused Oliver, "it would become a story people told. Maybe even a legend, about a witch, and some kids who disappeared."

"Eaten alive, no doubt," said Ms. Goolagong. "Let's move on."

They passed over more hills, and through a clearing with wildflowers in it, until the trees opened up and a field presented itself. A seven-thirty-looking field, with long shadows on it and clouds.

And there was Moo's house, in the middle distance. Past a familiar-looking fence, beyond the road.

But Moo didn't speed up, or look eager, or look nervous or pensive or any of the other things she should have looked. Instead she stopped and said, *Something isn't right.*

They stopped.

Something's missing.

Turning to Amy, she said, *Where are the cows?*

Ms. Goolagong was squinting around her in a suspicious kind of way.

"Something *isn't* right," she said. "I can feel it. We haven't . . . landed . . . where we meant to. *When* we meant to. Something has pulled us off course, you might say. Like accidentally taking the wrong highway exit."

The air cooled just a little more.

A faint rumbling, far off. Thunder?

No. A lone truck came growling down the road. A big truck.

Growling more loudly than most trucks. Going faster, too.

Ms. Goolagong stepped up between the girls, shading her eyes, watching the truck with interest.

"Perhaps we *didn't* miss," she declared, eyes blazing. "In fact, perhaps we've landed exactly where we aimed for. Gertrude mentioned her cows. It seems I remember a good deal of shouting about cows as we were launching ourselves into the time stream."

She bent down to look straight into Moo's eyes.

"Gertrude June," she said. "Amy Wood. You were thinking of your wonderful, free, wild, happy cows as we took off. Yes?"

Moo nodded.

"By chance," continued Ms. Goolagong, "were you also thinking of the truck accident you told me about?"

Moo shuffled her feet.

I couldn't help it, she said. *I think about that a lot. It's a big part of their history.*

"My confusion specifications have been exceeded again," said Oliver.

Ms. Goolagong straightened up, a knowing look in her eye.

"In any case," she said, "I feel that somehow we ourselves and time itself have conspired to place us exactly where—*when*—we are supposed to be."

The big truck had vanished behind a low hill. It came into view again, much closer and traveling much faster. It began to wobble somewhat, leaning one way and then the other. Had the driver fallen asleep?

"Oh no!" Oliver was saying. "Slow down!"

Brakes *screeeeeeeeeeeeeeeeeeech*ed . . . but it was too late.

The truck went down like a wounded animal, pitching over sideways, digging into the earth. Amy perceived a symbolic storm cloud all around it, stabbing lightning.

"NO!" shrieked all three children.

"OLIVES!" crowed Tuba.

Amy had never seen a wreck before. She wanted to cover her eyes but felt frozen.

The truck smashed through the fence and twisted to a stop.

Amy became aware of a new sound on the air. Not a mechanical sound at all, but something more like voices.

"MOOOOOOOOOOOOOOOOOOOO!" the voices were saying.

It's THEM! shouted Moo. *It's my cows! It's them, it's them, it's THEM!*

She started across the field, but Ms. Goolagong stopped her with a long, firm hand.

What? shouted Moo, struggling. *It's my COWS!*

"The driver might be hurt!" Amy chimed in. "We should go help!"

"The driver's fine," said Ms. Goolagong. "I can sense it. So can you, if you try. Now, just wait. Just watch. Let things happen."

Sure enough, the driver—a skinny man with long blond hair and a baseball cap—climbed out through the passenger door as if it were a submarine hatch. He was a mess: hair wrapped all over his face and neck, glasses askew, shirt ripped. But he was alive.

"He looks okay," said Amy.

There they are, said Moo, pointing.

A cow came trotting out into the road. She looked startled and inconvenienced but unhurt.

"MOOOOOO!" yelled Moo to this cow.

"MOOOOOO!" the cow yelled back.

"Toooooooooooooooooba!" squawked Tuba.

A second cow followed, with a gash across one shoulder. She hopped over the shattered remains of the fence, into the field. A third cow followed, and another, until an entire herd filled the roadside, the ditch, and the fringes of the pasture.

Tuba flew into the air, glided across the field, and landed gracefully on the hips of the biggest, brownest cow of them all.

The cow tossed her head and ogled him, and seemed about to swish him with her tail or buck him into the air, but changed her mind.

"Hi," said the bird to the cow. That's all he said. No speeches. No complaints. No lists. His emoji seemed to be trying to catch sunlight on its tongue.

The cow gave something like a shrug and snacked on some grass.

The driver clambered down into the weeds and hobbled as fast as he could along the length of the truck.

"HEY!" he shouted at the cows. "Hey, get back here!"

He's trying to keep them from wandering off, said Moo, *so he can finish taking them to the hamburger factory.*

Ms. Goolagong wore a thoughtful expression.

"So talk to them," she suggested. "Call them."

Moo nodded. She got an intense, concentrating look on her face.

Amy decided to help.

Come here, she thought at the cows.

More cows stumbled out of the truck. Some looked dazed, some were cut and slightly bloody, and some limped, but they all looked whole. They also looked glad to be alive and out of the truck.

Come here! Amy broadcast. *Ooooooooover heeeeeere!*

You're doing it wrong, said Moo, still concentrating.

"There's a right and wrong way to think stuff at cows?"

You're thinking words, Moo told Amy. *They don't know words. Think cow stuff at them.*

Okaaaaaaaaaaaaaay . . . cow stuff. Amy closed her eyes and sent summer daydreams across the field.

Grass. Milk. Baby cows. Warm sun. A breeze to keep flies away.

("What's going on?" asked Oliver, and Ms. Goolagong filled him in.)

Open meadows. Bright moons. Cool, fresh water. Yellow wildflowers.

The cows drifted toward the woods. Many of them lifted their heads, ears twitching, as if listening. Tuba rose into the air again and seemed to be trying to coax them along.

"MooooOOOOoOoooooooOOOOooooooo," he sang. "MoooOOOOOOOOOOOoooo!"

"[TOTALLY UNSUITABLE WORD]!" bawled the truck driver. He did his best to keep up with the cows, but his leg was having a bad day. He pushed and shoved, trying to turn them around, but they weren't having it.

"Back up some," said Ms. Goolagong. "Stay out of sight."

They did as she said, still calling to the cows.

Sweet hay. The warmth of other cows. Taking a nice, hot poop in an open field.

The cows were trotting now. The driver limped along, falling behind, shouting.

There's a guy who's probably going to get in a lot of trouble, thought Amy.

As she thought this, the cows stopped trotting and surged across the field at a full run.

"Um," said Amy.

"Something spooked them," remarked Ms. Goolagong.

No, said Moo. *They're not scared; they're happy. Look at their symbols!*

She was right, Amy saw. Over every bovine head bobbed a bright spinning heart, or a rainbow, or a pink sunburst. Even the limping cows, in the rear, were obviously wild with joy and freedom.

Which was wonderful and nice, but it occurred to Amy that the cows, in their happiness and enthusiasm, were picking up speed and getting uncomfortably close.

"Um," she said.

"Um indeed," replied Ms. Goolagong. "Perhaps if we jog over behind this convenient tree here . . ."

They didn't jog; they ran, all of them following the witch back toward the woods and then huddling behind a thick, proud old walnut tree.

"It would be a shame and an embarrassment," said Oliver, "to survive everything else and then be crushed by happy cows."

A moment later, the herd came thundering past,

smashing through leaves and underbrush. For a short time, the universe was a moo-storm of hooves and horns, rolling eyes and rainbows, with the earth shaking and the atmosphere smelling like a barnyard.

"MooOOOOOooooOOOOoo!" said a lot of the cows as they flew by.

"Mooooooo!" answered Moo.

"Mooooooo!" answered Amy and Oliver and Ms. Goolagong.

And then the stampede was past, pounding away through the trees, receding, leaving the humans behind in a great mess of smashed-up woods, saying "My goodness!" and "Wow!" to each other.

Halfway across the field, the driver stood scratching his ear and looking defeated. Over his head, a rain cloud poured, and flashed lightning.

He turned and hobbled away. Toward the dead truck and . . . ? Who knew what his plans were after that?

Moo mentally cleared her throat and said, *Let's go home. I don't want to stay around here and see if the hamburger people come and try to round up my cows.*

"I suspect someone will try," said Ms. Goolagong. "But I think we know they won't be successful."

They *did* know that, didn't they? thought Amy. Booyah!

"Nevertheless," Ms. Goolagong said, "Gertrude is quite correct; it's time we were going."

They began making their way through the trees, back toward the pond and the clock machine. The sun grew a tiny bit fatter and redder and lower in the sky.

The wind sighed. Branches creaked. Away through the woods somewhere, cows lowed and smashed around in the brush, still joyful, still broadcasting happy thoughts.

A dark, feathery shadow came flapping, fluttering, out of the sky and hitched a ride on Amy's shoulder.

His emoji was a thousand-watt lightbulb.

"The electric company thinks I'm made out of money," he said.

THROUGH THE TREES. OVER fallen branches, around great boulders. Down small valleys and up hills . . .

Amy's thoughts had left the present behind already, and she found herself getting mentally ready for the future, for home. She wanted quite badly to see Mom and Dad. She even kind of wanted to see Moo's mom. And *something* was going to happen with the Big Duke. What? Was it going to be dangerous? Her stomach clenched. She found that she was afraid of this mystery. Would Moo be able to help? Would Moo's mom even let her go to the field with the red X? Maybe if Amy asked super nicely. Should she explain about being able to hear Moo in her head? Would Moo's mom feel left out if—

Amy gasped.

She clutched at Moo's elbow and said, "OMG! MOO!"

WHAT? Moo, startled, stopped and glanced around to see what was wrong.

"OMG, Moo, I know how you can talk to your mom!"

Loud Girl! I thought something was about to eat us.

"Sorry."

Fine. Let's keep moving; I want to get there. Okay, so . . . ?

"You can read, right? You can understand words people say, and you can read, but you just can't say words or put them on paper?"

Moo nodded. *I can* decode, she said, *but I can't* encode. *That's how the doctors explained it.*

"Well, is there anything to keep you from pointing to letters in an alphabet? Or pictures, like if you had a big book full of pictures of all kinds of stuff?"

The idea interested and excited Moo; Amy could feel it.

I don't know. I could try.

She sounded hopeful. Amy liked that.

I've been thinking about it, too, said Moo. *Experimenting in my head, like you said. I also think I can do a lot—like, a LOT—with gesturing and acting things out, now that I can move.*

She sounded sooooo hopeful. Amy almost hugged her.

Don't hug me. Let's just get there, get there, get there. . . .

And then they were passing Ms. Goolagong's cabin and

descending the hillside toward the pond, toward the waiting clock machine.

I have something to confess, said Moo.

Amy looked at her sideways.

Every time we get up on this chair, it scares the absolute mrrzzl out of me.

Amy said, "I thought it was just me."

"People would get along quite a lot better," Ms. Goolagong said, "if they knew how much alike they all are inside."

Amy thought about that while they all climbed into the rocking chair. Just like before: Oliver and the girls in the witch's lap, with her strong arms holding them tight.

The clock . . . , said Moo.

"The clock is still set for home," said Amy. "But let's make sure we're focused. Think about home."

Amy closed her eyes and said, "Italian sausage and green peppers."

Hoofbeats drew closer. The ground shook. Little objects all over the chair began to quiver, tinkle, and vibrate. At the same time, a faint green glow began to pulse through the wood, through the wires.

My porch, said Moo.

"School."

My cows. My twenty-five-years-from-now cows.

"Mom and Dad pretending that I had died and that I smelled bad."

The road in front of my house.

"Cows!" said Amy.

I already said—

"No, I mean here and now! Look!" Amy grabbed Moo's chin and turned her head to face uphill, where an infinity of happy, frothing, stampeding cows had appeared, boiling and mooing toward them, wild with rainbows.

Amy whipped around in the chair.

"Concentrate, girls!" advised Ms. Goolagong. "Go now! Go, go, gogogogo!"

The cows weren't quite on top of them yet, but they would be in a moment.

Amy and Moo held hands and squinched their eyes closed.

"Shoplifting!" cried Amy.

My mom! cried Moo.

The cows made an effort to go around them, passing on the left.

MooOOOoooOOO! SPLASH! RUMBLE RUMBLE RUMBLE! A galaxy of noise and smells. The ground heaved under the chair.

"My tent!" wailed Amy. "My experiments!"

My cow mask!

"My friend Moo!" roared Amy.

My friend Amy! roared Moo.

Suddenly the chair was tilting, falling, jostled on one

side by a big, happy cow with black and white spots all over. Amy grabbed for Moo, for the back of the chair, for anything that would keep her from going over the side. Beside her, Moo poked desperately at the rabbit bell and missed.

The next instant, all four of them were in the air, flying and tumbling.

Amy came back down in the chair. Moo followed, landing across her lap.

SPLASH! Oliver and Ms. Goolagong came down in the pond.

"Oh NOOOOOOOOOO!" Amy cried.

NOOOOOOOO! shrieked Moo.

CRACK! Amy did not see the horn that sideswiped her head, but she heard it.

Loud, she mused.

The world all around was blurry and painful and glowing and green.

They fell through a hole in the world, and fell. . . .

28. AN INCREASED SENSITIVITY TO LIGHT

"WE'RE STILL FALLING," said Amy to Moo.

Her voice was stretchy and odd, as if she were speaking in rubber bands. It sounded like: "Wee**EE**Ee'RRRe still fffffAaaaaaaaaaaaAAAALLlll**llinggg**. . . ."

Not unlike a didgeridoo, Amy thought, and even her thoughts were stretchy.

MaaaayyyyyyyBBBbbbeeEE iiiiiittttttt'sss diffffffffffffffff-eeerrrrreeennNNNNNnTTttttt, replied Moo (who LOOKED stretchy and blurry, as if she were a flashlight being waved around), *goooooOOOoooing baaaaaack toooooowwwaaAAAArrrRRRRDDddd thhhhhe ffffuuuuu-UUUuuutttuurrrrreee.*

"NooOOoo," said Amy, whose head throbbed and felt wet and bloody. "SommmMMmethiiiing's wronnnNNnng."

Indeed! What *wasn't* wrong? Oliver and Ms. Goolagong had been knocked into the pond and were entirely gone, for one thing.

Iiiit'sss okaaaay, said Moo. *They're okaaaaaaay. I saw them get up and moooove awaaaaay from the cowsssssss. It's the last thing I saaaaaaw. . . .*

Okay. Well, that was the important thing. Still, Amy's heart gave a painful, sad stab.

For now, though, she sensed, it was important to figure out what else was wrong. The chair seemed to wobble in a way that didn't seem right. They had been pushed and thumped and almost smooshed, after all, and the poor chair seemed to have started coming apart here and there.

Indeed, as Amy thought these thoughts, the arm on her side came away in her right hand.

"Mrrzzzzzzzzzzzzzl," she said, feeling woozy.

Put it baaaack, said Moo. *You haaave to fiiiiiix it.*

"I knoooow," said Amy. "I will. Just gimme a miiiiinute."

Whatever had happened to her head was catching up with her. Maybe a little nap . . .

Moo shook her.

Amy fought off dizziness and struggled to fit the arm back where it belonged. There were these spindles and pegs, and some holes they fit into, except they weren't fitting.

Moo leaned over to help. *KERCHUNK!* The arm popped into place, strong and sturdy.

There, said Moo. *Now you can pass out.*

"'Kay," said Amy. But an instant later she got a funny feeling, like when you are in a car that takes a curve really fast and smooshes you up against the door, and then—

POW! Leaves leavesleaves and FLYING THROUGH THE AIR and LANDING ("Ow!") on her back and rolling (Ow! *Hello?!*) and leaves leavesleavesleaves . . .

And lying there in the leaves, near the pond, with birds flying by and gray clouds scooting overhead.

We're back, said Moo, close by.

Amy finally managed to pass out without getting interrupted.

AMY AWOKE TO A dull throb at the side of her head and an old woman hovering over her.

"Ms. Goolagong," she whispered. Of course.

"Welcome home," said the witch.

Her queenly hair was a gray waterfall now. She might have shrunk a little bit; it was hard to say. Certainly, she still had that tall *feeling* about her, but it seemed that her shoulders stooped somewhat and . . . well. She had, generally, the same old-people look that most old people have. Sort of like she needed a fresh coat of paint, but also wise and twinkly and comfortable.

Amy's head felt hot and sore. She raised a hand to her temple, and her fingertips encountered cloth, as if her head were wearing a big sock.

Ms. Goolagong brought bandages and some kind of cream, said Moo, leaning into view on Amy's other side. *She saw the cow hit you when we took off, and figured you'd need doctoring of some kind.*

"I've had twenty-five years to think about what you might need," said the witch. "And I obviously thought it out just right."

"I'm not dying?" asked Amy, trying to sit up. "Am I paralyzed or concussed or brain damaged?"

Moo and the witch helped her sit up.

"You can stand when you feel like it," said Ms. Goolagong. "No, you're not any of those things. If you were concussed, your eyes would be goofy or there'd be other signs. Besides, I can tell." She waggled her fingers in the air, witch-magic-style.

Amy recalled the witch coming over the hill as they took off, that first time, aboard the chair. Back when they assumed she was a witchier witch. A *bad* witch, presumably.

It occurred to her that Ms. Goolagong—this older version of Ms. Goolagong—had actually just *now* seen them leave. Seen them launch. Or vanish or whatever.

"Why were you shouting 'No'?" Amy asked her.

Ms. Goolagong looked puzzled. She said, "Hmm?"

"I remember when we were about to whoosh away through time," said Amy, "you were coming over the hill, running at us, yelling, 'No!'"

That's right, said Moo. *That's true.*

The witch laughed. She reached out and laid a hand on Amy's shoulder.

"'*Go,*'" she said. "Not 'no.' I was hollering at you to *go*, because . . . well, it looked like you were hesitating, or having difficulty, and at the same time, you were arriving, back from the past. I don't know what would happen if all four of you were stuck here in the same time-space together. Not to mention that if you didn't leave in the first place, you couldn't very well be returning. It just seemed best if you went ahead and left, so I yelled at you to go. It seems to have worked out."

The girls agreed.

"But," said Amy, "twenty-five years! You got knocked out of the chair and stuck back in time! It's not what was supposed to happen!"

Ms. Goolagong laughed and shrugged. "Who's to say,"

she said, "what's supposed to happen? We're all here finally. We're all fine, more or less."

"Oliver?"

"Fine, more or less. Don't you worry about Oliver just now. Worry about *now.*"

It was amazing, Amy reflected, the things that seemed possible now. In just a day or two, she had come to know so much more than she'd known before. She almost felt like a different person. Or a bigger version of the *same* person. Or . . . well, there would have to be experiments.

"So," said Amy. "We're home, then. Timewise."

Moo and Ms. Goolagong nodded.

Amy could feel it, actually. Her own time had its own feeling.

One time her parents had sent her off to her grand-mother's for half of a summer. When she had come home, it had been just slightly like entering a house for the first time. All the familiar things seemed new, just for a few seconds—the carpet in the hall, the smell of the kitchen, her own room, neat and clean—and then the familiarity had come flooding back, like comfortable clothes you had worn six thousand times. This, *now,* was like that.

New and familiar. And wonderful.

Together the three of them surveyed what was left of the clock machine, which was quite destroyed. Amy glimpsed a cameo and the rabbit bell half buried in twigs. Here and there, at impressive distances, lay parts of the chair.

Noticing this debris, Amy was not too tired to notice a few other things. Like differences in the trees . . . Over here, a tree that had been young and slender and not too tall thirty years ago was now wide and strong, with roots like a fortress. Over there, a gray stone the size of a tricycle had waaaay more moss growing on it.

Time passed and things changed. Amy felt suddenly aware of just how little time she had been alive, and how old the earth was. Old and constantly changing, like a river.

It hurts my brain, said Moo, *thinking about how old the earth is.*

"If that hurts your brain," said Ms. Goolagong, "think of how old the stars are, and the entire universe out there."

Amy didn't feel ready to try that just now. "Maybe later," she said. Now there were things that needed to be done.

At that moment, there was a fluttering in the air, and a large, gray, somewhat shipwrecked-looking bird came in for a landing on Ms. Goolagong's shoulder.

Almost crashed but didn't quite.

The bird—it was Tuba, of course—steadied himself and said, "I swear I've spent a year of my life sitting here watching this dumb computer buffering, buffering, buffering."

Amy and Moo told him, "Hi!"

"I can't remember if I changed my underwear," he replied.

THEY ALL HIKED UPHILL to the old cabin, which sat rotting and leaning sideways, propped up on one end by a young tree.

Ms. Goolagong sighed a little, and they passed on by, headed for the edge of the woods.

Amy told the witch she was kind of surprised to find Tuba still alive.

"Hearsay birds can live a long time," said Ms. Goolagong. "Sometimes he goes out and socializes with the cows, but mostly he sleeps the day away."

This was sooooo strange, Amy kept thinking. How often did you say goodbye to someone who was (just a guess) thirty-five or so years old, and then ten minutes later you were hiking through the trees with them and they were sixty-five?

The answer was: not often.

"Where's Oliver?" she asked.

Ms. Goolagong nodded, as if she found this to be a good question, asked at just the right time. They kept walking, and while they walked, the witch told them the story of the twenty-five years they had just flown through on the clock machine.

Except it wasn't really a story, as such.

"It's not really a story," she said, looking off into space, as if focusing on something distant or long ago. "Which is a surprise. You think, when you are very young, that your life is going to be a story, with a beginning and a middle and, sadly, an end. And it IS. But when you get far enough along, you look back and it's mostly feelings you remember."

They passed over a familiar-looking dead tree, blanketed in moss.

"I remember feeling terrified living with Oliver at first, because I'd never been a mother or a father before, and suddenly I was both. At the same time, I remember feeling like I was waking up, because so much was new suddenly. We bought a secondhand camper and went from place to place. I played a lot of different roles, like sometimes working in a library for a while—we had to have money, after all—and also being Oliver's science teacher and his math teacher and his school nurse and his basketball coach and . . ."

She waved her hand dismissively, saying, "You get the picture."

They passed between some boulders. They frightened a chipmunk, which scrabbled away and sat out of sight, scolding them. Tuba, still perched on Ms. Goolagong's shoulder, woke up long enough to say "Wrinkle cream" to the chipmunk.

"Oliver did as most children do," said the witch. "Got older and left. College. Law school. Jobs and cars and girlfriends and boyfriends and moving far away. So I've been living this chapter for a while where it's just me again. I remember there was a comet in the sky once, for three months. I got a job at a museum in the city, working in a laboratory. I met a man named James, a librarian, and we married, and we lived in the city together, and then we unmarried. I wrote a book of poems and collected mushrooms. I have begun to shrink somewhat. Gravity does that. My eyes suffer from an increased sensitivity to light. Beyond that, I am enjoying having arrived at old age with all four limbs and most of my senses intact. Would you like to hear one or more of my poems? Amy, I think you might like this:

"I am flying high
But . . . I'm not a bird! Oh no!
Aaaaaaaaaaaaaaaaaaaaaah! Thud."

Neither Amy nor Moo knew quite what to say.

"It's a haiku," Ms. Goolagong explained.

"It's . . . interesting," said Amy. "But I don't think it's a haiku."

"Five, seven, five," argued Ms. Goolagong.

"'Aaaaaaaaah!' isn't five syllables. I mean, it could be,

but . . ." She trailed off because Ms. Goolagong was waving her hand—her long, veiny hand—impatiently.

"How about this, then:

"What does winter do in July?
I'll tell you what he does. He goes fishing, like
Anyone else. He haunts creeks and ocean shores
And avoids bookstores and Kentucky Fried
    Chickens,
Where he tends to leave embarrassing puddles."

Amy brightened. "Oh!" she said. "Well, that's better! That's good! Isn't it, Moo?"

I guess, said Moo.

"See," said Ms. Goolagong, "because when he's at the ocean or fishing in a creek, he's already in the water, so when he melts a little, it's not—"

We get it.

"It's beautiful," said Amy. "You should set it to didgeridoo music."

"So I should. Or maybe I already did. Can't quite remember."

Ms. Goolagong's eyes had taken on a distant look, Amy noticed, and her voice had started to sound far away. As if her thoughts were someplace else.

The light changed. The woods around them were thinning, and, through the trees, Amy glimpsed the pasture ahead, populated by a cow or two.

She realized that Ms. Goolagong had stopped and dropped behind. The girls stopped, too, and turned to look at her.

Wow. She sure looks witchy, they thought. *So beautiful.*

"You girls have work to do," said Ms. Goolagong. "Both of you. Go do it."

And she pointed with her chin at the world beyond the woods.

You can come with us, said Moo, *you know.*

"What," said Amy, "are you going back to your *house,* with the tree growing in it and—"

"God's teeth, no!" cried the old woman. "There must be germs in there big enough to swallow me whole; I haven't lived there for decades. My home is a hundred times snazzier than that, and I've got to get back and check on my pies. Now go on. Don't say anything. Just go."

So they didn't say goodbye. They simply put one foot in front of the other, marching through an afternoon full of wind and blowing leaves.

THE PASTURE. COWS. AND Moo's house.

This time no trucks came barreling down the road. Nothing interrupted the girls' march across the field, escorted by their big, four-legged friends.

Then something did interrupt. It was Moo herself, stopping short, suddenly gasping.

Um, she said.

"Um?" said Amy.

Moo grabbed Amy's hands, squeezing.

Walking, she said. *Me walking and moving around on my own is going to be big news for my mom. The doctors always told her it was a possibility, but it's still going to be a surprise. Maybe even a shock. What if she has a conniption and dies? It happens.*

"I think she'll be very happy," said Amy. "That's all."

Maybe I should wait a few days. Pretend it's happening slowly. Or maybe—

The sound of a door creaking open and banging shut.

They looked across the street, and there was Moo's mom taking the trash out. Looking more than ever like something that had gone through the wash too many times, she shuffled down the broken concrete walk, carrying a plastic kitchen bag in each hand.

MOM! bellowed Moo, jumping up and down, waving like a windmill.

(*So much for caution,* thought Amy.)

"Ms. Kopernikus!" she shouted, trying to help.

MOM! MOM, MOMMOMMOMMOMMOM!

Moo's mom looked up, blinked expressionlessly, and

dropped both bags onto the walk, where they tore open and spilled.

Moo was over the fence, across the road without looking at ALL, across the grass without really touching down, it seemed, and then she was jumping up—

And her mother caught her, and didn't drop her, and they were standing there like that, like some old pajamas holding a ball of fire.

By the time Amy had crossed the road and stepped over the garbage, Moo was back on the ground, and the two of them stood holding hands.

Moo's mom—Ms. Kopernikus—glanced at Amy but then went back to staring at her daughter as if she couldn't take her eyes off her.

"What happened?" asked Ms. Kopernikus. "It's . . . it's so wonderful. The doctors said maybe someday, but . . ." She trailed off.

Amy shrugged. "It's a mystery," she said. "I think maybe something startled her, or her neurons woke up, or—"

I love you, said Moo, *but don't you have somewhere to be? Let me do this.*

Moo wanted this particular scene to herself.

Oh, said Amy. *Oh sure. Of course.*

"Moo—Gertrude—can tell you herself," she told Ms. Kopernikus. "One way or another." (Indeed, Amy saw,

Moo's hands and arms were already twitching, as if dying to start gesturing and talking and explaining and making things *happen*!)

Ms. Kopernikus raised her eyebrows and said how wonderful that would be. She was like a TV picture that was slowly changing from black and white to color. Her eyes, for the first time in Amy's memory, looked like there was an actual person inside. Above her head, hearts kept swelling up and popping like balloons.

"Your head's bleeding," said Ms. Kopernikus, reaching out and not quite touching Amy's bandage. "Maybe you should come inside and—"

"It *was* bleeding," Amy said. "But a helpful grown-up like yourself applied direct pressure and things, and also applied this bandage. Thanks, though. My mom's going to look at it. She's expecting me."

Ms. Kopernikus blinked and said, "Oh. Well then, okay. Good."

Amy gave Moo a quick hug, darted across the yard, retrieved her bike from the grass, and rolled—

"Amy!" called Ms. Kopernikus. "I'm not sure going down to the field right now is such a hot idea, hon. That ridiculous machine must have kept moving overnight; it's much closer now."

Aw. Moo's mom was looking out for her. That was good and felt nice.

"It's okay," Amy replied, waving. "I'll be triple-super-extra careful!"

And off she went, down the road, into a wind like horses, ahead of an approaching dusk like a storm at sea.

AMY PASSED THROUGH THE woods, and when the trees opened up on the other side, she hit her brakes and put her feet down and wobbled to a halt.

There was the Big Duke, towering over the field like a cross between a factory and a dragon. Up and down its ponderous metal arm, thick cables whizzed and snapped. At the end of the arm, its humongous claw—a great wheel with massive scooping teeth—turned ponderously.

And there were her parents, standing defiantly right underneath it.

All sorts of feelings and electricities ran through Amy then. Fears and superpowers. Time and science and magic.

Was she brave enough for this?

A whirlwind of thought and memory sang in her head. It carried her parents and the giant love they had for her. It carried Moo and Oliver, who had so much to overcome but never, ever gave up. And Ms. Goolagong! If the earth and the wind and stars had a soul, it was Ms. Goolagong. They were all people who took what they loved and believed in and went out and did something with it, no matter what.

Could she be like that? It was time to find out.

"MRRZZL!" she roared. *"This is a bravery experiment!"* And she charged forth on her bike, butterfly hood laced tight, antennae shooting invisible battle rays.

29. THE BIG DUKE

HER PARENTS WEREN'T ALONE, Amy saw, ditching her bike and running toward the camp. A police officer was with them, and another man. A thick man in a suit, wearing a fur coat and a hat.

"I can't make them move if they don't care to," the cop was saying.

The cop appeared, Amy thought, to be a police captain or general or something. He had a gold badge, and fancy braids and decorations splashed all over his uniform.

"This is public land," he continued, addressing the man in the fur coat. "You hold mineral rights. If they were underground, they'd be trespassing. THEN I could make them move, or even arrest them. But they're not underground, see?"

Amy squinted at the police chief's face. How old was he? Sixty? Fifty-five? Sixty-five? Man, over thirty, they all looked the same.

"That's the dumbest thing I ever heard," said Fur Coat. "Now, you listen to me, Byrd. It costs thirty thousand big ones a day just to keep the Duke's engine running. Not to mention . . ."

Byrd? Amy thought. *Officer Byrd?*

If she squinted just right, she could make the years melt away, could see the young truant officer inside this sixty-year-old veteran.

Officer Byrd had become chief of police. Or general or admiral or whatever.

Well, good. He was doing a fine job.

Fur Coat was still talking.

". . . last thing I'm willing to stand here and tolerate is these two hacks making rabbit eyes at us when we're ready to [unsuitable word—a BIG one!]"—Amy's ears popped— "DIG!"

"Calm down, Henry," said Chief Byrd in a certain voice you sometimes hear from cops and teachers and maybe the president.

And Fur Coat calmed down. Or at least shut up.

Henry?

It couldn't be.

Amy squinted. No . . .

Yes. There he was, inside the meat-chop face, under the dumb hat, tucked away behind years of whatever made a person thick like that.

It was Henry Zane.

Henry Zane had become a big-shot mining dude of some kind.

"Amy," said someone.

It was Mom.

Mom turned and left the red X, walked over, and leaned down to speak to her, close up.

"Hi, Offspring," she said, twisting her pinkie ring a mile a minute. "Listen, it won't help us if you're right here where it's dangerous. You're very brave—that's no secret—but for now we need you to help us out by staying away. I want you to go back to Moo's house and stay . . . *What happened to your head?*"

"I bumped it on a chair. It's okay. . . . Mom! It's okay! Trust me, okay? Please, you can fuss about me later, I promise."

Mom bent down and hugged her really hard. Amy hugged her back.

Then Amy said, "Go save the world!"

"Yes, ma'am, Offspring. Jeez! Anyway, stay with Moo until one of us comes to get you. Promise."

Amy promised. Then she turned and rolled her bike back the way she had come.

She wouldn't go all the way to Moo's probably. Mom and Dad would be happy enough if she just got away from the camp. It would be okay, probably, if she just watched from the road, by the woods. If her parents were going to be on the news or something, being braver than any twenty people, she had a right to see it firsthand.

She would also see it firsthand if things went badly or got stupid, and her parents wound up getting mined and chopped and crushed by that giant toothy wheel. Which was still moving, if slowly.

Amy remembered the people who had crowded around them at the pond, with their torches and rocks. People didn't always think about what they were doing. Sometimes people did awful things just by being there and being angry.

Her stomach tightened, and she felt a bit sick.

At the same time, she noticed something like a storm cloud forming over the campsite, over the X and the Big Duke.

It was a symbol of bad things about to happen. It was clear and plain and obvious, if you could read things like Amy could.

Behind her, a branch went *snap*.

Amy wheeled around. Who was there? It was people from town, come to throw things and call her parents names!

No, it wasn't.

It was Moo and her mom, holding hands, picking their way through the weeds, out into the field. Moo had her hood up and her head down, watching her step, so that her great plastic eyes (full of battle science and earth magic!) regarded Amy fiercely (in a cow kind of way).

Mom says that if something unexpected doesn't happen, your parents are going to get either smashed or arrested.

"Your parents are brave people," said Ms. Kopernikus. "They always have been."

Amy started to say "Thanks," but Moo's mom knelt down, just then, to face her daughter.

She kissed Moo between her cow eyes.

Amy heard Moo say, *Be careful. Be careful. Be careful. Becarefulbecarefulbecareful. . . .*

Then Ms. Kopernikus walked away across the dirt and the broken cornstalks, toward the knot of grown-ups on the red X.

Moo reached over and gently lifted Amy's chin and helped her close her mouth, which had dropped open.

Moo's mom stood with Mom and Dad.

"Your mom's a hippie," observed Amy.

My mom's a warrior, said Moo, *like your mom and dad. She just forgot for a while.*

They held hands.

SLAM! A car door, out on the road.

Noises from the roadside.

Amy looked over to see people getting out of cars.

She lifted her lip and made a face at them. She couldn't help it.

People from town. Some of them were laughing. Big fat surprise.

"Hippies!" someone called out. "Hippies, go on home. Let people work! You know: work?"

("My parents are *scientists*!" Amy wanted to shout. "People like them make *everything* possible!")

No. She would be silent. This was her parents' fight.

Something made a lot of noise, approaching from out of sight, beyond the woods.

The noise went *WUBBAWUBBAWUBBAWUBBA-WUBBAWUBBA* and made the whole atmosphere vibrate. A news helicopter appeared over the trees. It advanced, maybe a hundred feet in the air, circling.

More cars pulled off the road.

Some people got out and took pictures of the Big Duke. Amy could hear them saying, "Wow-wee!" and "Lookit that thing!" as if it were designed to spit out pumpkin pies instead of poison the water and soil.

They were shouting now, out there on the big red X.

The red X, Amy now saw, had a spirit. Or rather, the ground beneath it did.

An open wound.

Over by the cars, there was movement. Someone advancing through the weeds. Someone marching across the field with a club in one hand.

Amy's mouth hung open again.

Was that person mad enough to go out there and start hitting her mom and dad with things?

No way! Amy started forward, and so did Moo.

But it wasn't someone going out there to hit and yell and be mad and mean. Amy squinted, and—

"It's Mrs. Barch!" she gasped.

And so it was.

Mrs. Barch wasn't carrying a club. She had a plain old stick and simply used it to steady herself as she crossed the uneven ground.

"Come on!" called Amy, grabbing Moo's hand. And the two of them ran up behind Mrs. Barch and took her by the elbows.

"Goodness!" said Mrs. Barch (she was old again, of course, with a scratchy voice). "Amy Wood! Thanks, girls. Well, Amy, your parents have got spunk, I'll give them that. They're right, too, and more people than you know find themselves in agreement. Look at that Henry Zane boy out there. No big surprise. Poor kid never had a chance."

Mrs. Barch looked down at Moo, squinted, and said, "You're that Kopernikus girl, aren't you?"

Moo nodded.

"You're better," observed Mrs. Barch.

Moo nodded.

"Well, good. Good! Then I'll expect you at school tomorrow, if we're all lucky enough to stay out of jail and not get chopped up."

They reached the X and left Mrs. Barch with the other grown-ups.

Heading back toward the woods, they—

*GRRrRRRRRRRUM**MMMBBBBUUMMM-BBBUUUUBBBUUB**!*

Behind them, above them, such a noise! Louder than the news helicopter!

It was the Big Duke's clawed wheel. It was coming down faster all of a sudden, and it was turning as if something had flicked a monstrous on switch. It spun slowly at first, but quickly picked up speed—VROOOOOOOOOOOOOO**OOOOOOOOOOOO**!—gears gnashing, cables screaming, until the digging wheel was a blur, a hurricane of iron teeth zeroing in on the exact . . . middle . . . of . . . the . . . X.

Zeroing in on Mom and Dad and Moo's mom and Mrs. Barch and Chief Byrd.

Not Henry Zane, though. He was GONE like a track star, sprinting for safety.

"Get that thing SHUT DOWN!" he shrieked into a walkie-talkie as he shot past Amy and Moo. "WHO IN HELL GAVE THE ORDER TO ENGAGE THE GANTRY ARM?"

The walkie-talkie protested, saying that no one had touched nothin', that the thing had just started up and WOULDN'T SHUT OFF, and Amy's whole body went cold, and then Henry Zane was too far away to be heard, over by the road, watching in horror like everyone else as the terrible wheel kept chewing downward.

Chief Byrd was trying to move everyone off the X.

Mom and Dad and Moo's mom and Mrs. Barch weren't having it, though.

Amy could hear what they were thinking.

I don't believe it, her mom and dad were saying in the privacy of their own heads. *It's a trick. They'll scare us off and then start digging for real.*

They looked at each other then, Mom and Dad did. Some kind of signal passed between them. Something Amy couldn't quite read. All she knew for sure was that the heart symbols over their heads suddenly grew ten times bigger and brighter.

Mom and Dad ripped off their shirts.

What? Why?

Underneath their plain, everyday shirts, they wore T-shirts reading KUNG and FOO in huge red letters.

Mom was Kung. Dad was Foo.

"No," said Amy, "way!"

Way, said Moo. *I knew it!*

"NO," repeated Amy, "WAY!"

Mom and Dad shut their eyes and kept on playing chicken with the giant wheel.

Except it *wasn't* a trap. It wasn't playacting by the mining company. The wheel was out of control; why didn't her parents see that?

The whole machine shook and rattled. In half a minute, maybe less, the churning wheel would descend on the X, and it would be like someone had thrown hamburger into a fan (*brrrraaaaaaaaaaaaappp!*—pieces of Mom and Dad, chunks of Mrs. Barch and Chief Byrd!).

"I think that's quite enough," said a voice that was like the cop/teacher/president voice mixed together with a sort of queenly tone, like a swan commanding an army.

If I need to tell you who it was, you haven't been paying attention.

She arrived from the direction of the road, like a sailing ship in a dark gown, gray hair flying like sails, with her mouth set like a trap that had snapped shut. She propelled herself with her didgeridoo on the left-hand side. On the right-hand side, she had help.

A familiar figure in a dark suit. With hair like a haystack. Hair like a whole entire farm. It was the odd stranger who had convinced Amy's parents not to give up and go home.

Amy squinted and subtracted years.

It was Oliver, of course.

Not boy Oliver, full of uncertainty and sadness, but an Oliver who looked like he knew quite well what he was about. Despite the hair, he had an aura of being confident and strong, even sort of shiny in his coat and tie and long, dark coat, the way a racehorse looks. A large, sleepy-looking gray bird perched (none too steadily) atop his head, but he still looked fine and good, despite this.

Ms. Goolagong stopped at the edge of the red X and pointed her didgeridoo at the deadly wheel and shouted—

BRAAAAAAAP! Iron teeth smashed the didgeridoo into matchsticks.

Ms. Goolagong seemed surprised, but only for a moment.

Then she just pointed up with her own finger and said, "STOP."

No, she didn't. She didn't say it.

Amy heard her think it. Heard her *command* it.

STOP, said Ms. Goolagong, and Amy could see her shaking. Not with fear, or because she was about to collapse, but because whatever percent of her was a witch, she was using 100 percent of it.

In the meantime, the other grown-ups had turned to observe the new arrivals. Chief Byrd looked concerned. Ms. Kopernikus looked curious. And Mom and Dad . . .

It was hard to tell what Mom and Dad were thinking and feeling. Amy reached out with her witch senses, stretching and listening. . . .

They were puzzled. They thought Ms. Goolagong looked familiar, and something about her frightened them.

It can't be her! Amy heard them thinking. *But it is!*

Amy wondered how many other people here had been in the woods thirty years ago, to see the witch vanish into thin air with three kids on her lap. How many of them had made themselves forget? How many had simply refused to believe what they had seen?

Ms. Goolagong was looking awfully witchy, scowling and gesturing at the Big Duke as if she could magic it to a stop with the powers of her mind.

Did they think she looked witchy, or maybe just kind of sad?

Her parents, Amy saw, had put off their confusion for the moment and were moving to help the strange woman. Old people needed help sometimes.

But the wheel slowed.

Buh-ROOOOOOOOOooooooooooooo . . .

"Yes!" cried Amy.

The wheel slowed, and slooooooowed . . . but it didn't stop.

Amy and Gertrude, said Ms. Goolagong. *Don't just stand there.*

Amy wanted to cry out that she was only half a percent of a witch, and that being able to see the healthy heart of an apple tree or the ghost stories in a patch of earth was not the same as being able to move things and reach into things and command them and change them . . . but she didn't say this.

Instead she *tried.*

The next thing she knew, she and Moo were reaching, reaching out with their whole selves, wanting the wheel to STOP, to BREAK! They squeezed and witched and pushed and became like a big cloud of invisible Play-Doh around the claws and cables and speed and *whizzzzzzzzz* . . . and the wheel slooooowed some more. . . .

But not enough.

Amy was so afraid, suddenly, that it was almost like a calm.

Inside the calm was an idea. A simple, sensible idea.

Sometimes, she said to Moo, *just because science is deep doesn't mean it can't be simple.*

Moo looked puzzled for a second, but then she saw the idea in Amy's head and nodded furiously.

With half the town watching, plus a lot of people in TV-land, Amy and Moo unzipped their hoodies and swung them over their heads.

The butterfly hoodie behaved like a sling, with something like twenty rocks and stones in its pockets. It whirled faster and faster. The cow hoodie did the exact same thing, spinning until it was a blur, like an airplane propeller.

Until Amy and Moo cried, *NOW!*—and sent the hoodies flying like arrows straight into the wheel.

Which ripped them to shreds. (Sad face.)

And choked on them.

KER-CHOOK! GRiiiiiiiiiiiiiiiiiiiiiiind! KERCHOOK! CRASH! CHOOKA!

Choked on rocks and stones from the woods and the school and the pond and everywhere.

Choked and—*CHOOKA PHZZzzzzzzzzzzzzzzzzz!*—died. (Happy face.)

The Big Duke started leaking black smoke here and there. It began to smell like burning rubber. Mining company people climbed down and ran into the field, holding on to their hard hats.

Mom and Dad and Moo's mom and Chief Byrd and Mrs. Barch all opened their eyes. Just one eye apiece at first, glancing one way and another.

"We're dead," said Mrs. Barch. "I can tell. Well, I never thought I'd be surrounded in heaven by a bunch of former students. Which, no offense, wouldn't have been my first choice. A big, fat glass of wine, on the other hand—"

"We're not dead," said Chief Byrd. "We're alive, and very lucky. It wouldn't have been my choice to be out here at ALL, except that I've got a whole town full of zealots and hippies and—"

"Shhhhh," said Ms. Goolagong.

"And witches," said Chief Byrd.

"Nothing was ever proven," argued Ms. Goolagong.

"It WAS you!" said Dad, stepping up.

"We SAW!" said Mom, beside him.

They were trying to sound confident, Amy could tell, but their eyes told a different story. They looked dreadfully, badly confused. They looked like they might start crying.

They looked at Ms. Goolagong (who said nothing), and they also looked at their own daughter and her friend Moo. And Ms. Kopernikus stepped up beside Mom, and she was looking at them funny, too. And looking puzzled.

They recognize us, said Moo.

Is that good or bad? asked Amy.

Hard to tell, said Ms. Goolagong. *They might just go mad. Give them a minute.*

(How would you explain it to yourself? Amy wondered.

Hey, I remember seeing this girl thirty years ago, even though she's only ten and I know for a FACT she wasn't born yet. . . .)

Mom turned to Dad, saying, with an unsteady giggle, "I always *thought* she looked familiar. . . ."

And with that, all three parents kind of collapsed onto the ground and sat there with their eyes wobbling around.

Amy and Moo left them alone for a while to get their minds wrapped around things, and paid attention to a separate drama happening about ten feet over THAT way.

Chief Byrd pointed a stern police finger across the cornfield. "Henry Zane!" he roared. "Get your [unsuitable word] over here!"

People had started walking over from the roadside, taking pictures. Of the broken machine looming over everything like a dead giant, and the serious-looking chief of police. They took pictures of the protesters sitting on the ground.

And they took pictures of Henry Zane as he came slinking back to the red X.

"Henry," said Chief Byrd, "this machine of yours is a menace."

Henry Zane wasn't quite as defeated as he'd seemed. He looked at Byrd with a fire in his eye and said, "Listen, you officious clown. If anyone was in danger, it was their own stupid fault for standing here right on the insertion mark when they knew darn well what was going to happen.

And yeah, the machine's got bugs. It has three million moving parts and at least five different electronic systems operating in tandem. Most of these idiots here"—he pointed all around at the townspeople—"can barely keep a car running. In any case, there's nothing to keep us from pouring some more money down its throat and getting back up to speed before the holidays. We'll be in the ground by December tenth, I'll betcha. Merry Christmas, everybody."

The crowd around Henry Zane made unfriendly noises, but you could tell he didn't care one bit. He knew very well what percentage of them were warriors, were likely to stand up to him in any real way, and that was almost zero percent. It was the kind of thing he counted on.

They didn't let him down. They walked away, taking pictures as they went.

"Mr. Zane?" said a voice. A different kind of voice.

It was Oliver's voice, Amy realized. His man voice.

"What?" seethed Henry Zane.

Oliver stepped forward, snapped open a briefcase, and handed the mining boss a sheaf of papers.

Henry Zane looked at the papers as if they might be poison, but he took them.

"What kind of nonsense—"

"Mr. Zane," said Oliver, "I represent the Eighth Federal Ecological Zoning Board, an agency certified by the United States Department of the Interior, as well as being under the auspices of the 2006 Paris environmental accords, et cetera and so forth. It is my pleasant duty to inform you that this land is the sole ecological support of one of only five herds of wild cows in the continental US. We have secured federal protection for these endangered animals and their habitat, and as such, this land now falls under the protection of the Endangered Species Act and is strictly off-limits to mining and any other industrial concerns, et cetera and so forth, legal language, legal words, et cetera."

Henry Zane's eyes were twitching. Both of them. You hardly ever see that.

"I wanna speak to your boss," he sneered.

"My boss is the president of the United States," said Oliver. "I can give you a number, but I doubt she'll take your call. She's busy doing work and things."

The hearsay bird on Oliver's head woke up long enough to say, "President of the United States," and then zonked out again.

Henry Zane looked like a slowly deflating balloon. There was a tiny symbol floating over his head, Amy saw. Something like . . . well, it was a piece of poop. Gross. If you looked closely, you could see that it *wanted* to be heart-shaped. It looked like it was *trying* but hadn't had much success so far.

There was a symbol over Oliver's head—his wild hay-stack head—something like a crown with a heart in it.

"MooOOOoooo!" said Moo to Henry Zane.

Henry Zane looked insulted, stuck out his tongue, and slumped away toward the road.

AMY SAT DOWN BETWEEN her mom and dad and said, "Hi."

They put their arms around her.

When people are feeling scared and uncertain, Amy knew, it was often a good idea to say some nice things to them.

"You guys are brave," she said. "AWFULLY brave."

Nothing.

Or you could give them something else to think about.

"By the way," she said, "*technically*, I still did what you told me to do. I wasn't on the X, so technically—"

"Shhhh," they said. "It's okay."

"Confusing," said Dad, "but I have faith that an explanation that makes some kind of sense—" His voice got shaky.

"Shhhh," Amy told him.

Moo sat down with her mom. They grinned at each other and shrugged.

Dad looked at Ms. Kopernikus and said, "Thanks, Heather."

"It's good to see you again," said Mom. "It's been a while."

Ms. Kopernikus managed to look happy and sort of sad at the same time. She said, "I know."

Moo, said Amy. *They called your mom Heather.*

Hello, I know my mom's name. Dur!

No, I mean . . . like Heather from the school and the woods. Little Heather, who—

OMG! said Moo, eyes bugging. *No way!*

Amy could see it in Ms. Kopernikus's face if she really tried. The small girl who was brave enough to kick and fight even when her arm was being twisted. She was *in* there!

NO, repeated Moo, *WAY!*

But she saw it. She slowly took her mom's hand and just sat there looking at her some more.

After a little while, Amy and her parents got up and started picking through their camp, which had been trampled. Amy saw a zillion packages of superdehydrogenated peas and carrots and Salisbury steak broken open and strewn among the cornstalks. Her own tent had been dragged around and stepped on.

"Anybody ready to go home?" Dad asked Mom, and they both looked at Amy.

"Hell yes," said Mrs. Barch, who nodded around at everyone and started crossing the cornfield with caution, probing ahead with her cane.

"Mrs. Barch," said Amy's mom, "would you care to—"

"Nope," said Mrs. Barch, not stopping. "I'm going home. You people scare me."

Amy was about to tell her mother yes, she'd like very

much to go home, but then a voice spoke up. A voice both tired and queenly.

"I wonder," said this voice, "if I might convince anyone to join me at my home for a warm slice of pondhouse pie. I daresay we would all like to sit and be comfortable for a spell. Besides, some of you might have questions. . . ."

Mom and Dad and Ms. Kopernikus looked a tad lost still. Looked like they weren't sure if they wanted to go to this woman's house and be made comfortable.

Ms. Goolagong stood like a grand old tree.

Oliver appeared at the witch's side and addressed the three parents.

"You'll find," he said, sounding crisp and bright, "that the things you've seen or think you saw, whether five minutes ago or thirty years—my goodness!—ago, make a great deal more scientific sense if you use your words and ask a question or two."

Mom and Dad and Ms. Kopernikus all spoke at once.

"Who *are* you?" they asked Ms. Goolagong.

"I'm Ms. Elaine Goolagong," she answered.

Mom's and Dad's foreheads furrowed. Then their eyes flew wide, startled.

"*The* Ms. Elaine Goolagong?" said Mom. "*Dr.* Elaine Goolagong?"

"The Elaine Goolagong who discovered the Peanut Galaxy?" said Dad.

"And the Rose Galaxy?" said Mom. "And galaxy NGC HG3784698?"

Ms. Goolagong, for once, was taken aback.

"Well, yes," she said.

Mom and Dad gushed and blushed, both competing to tell her that they worked at the university, where she was quite famous, and was it true about her husband, and so on. Because if *that* was true, maybe it wasn't so strange, the thing with the disappearing rocking chair, which they might or might not have seen long ago, and—

"So then," interrupted Ms. Goolagong. "Pie? My place? Yes?" And all three parents nodded as she gathered them with her long, mighty old hands and steered them gently toward the road.

"Excuse me?" Amy said, hopping up to tap the witch on the shoulder. "Your house? You haven't lived in that old cabin for years, and you said there were huge, man-eating germs, and—"

"Please," said Ms. Goolagong, turning toward the road. "I've got much better accommodations these days."

She waved one hand thataway, down the roadside. Amy looked, and there it was . . . Ms. Goolagong's house.

It was unmistakable.

The house was a bus, parked a hundred yards away. A school bus, perhaps, or an art festival on wheels. It was painted all over with great yellow stars and red comets. Plus moons and UFOs and peace signs and hearts and birds and rockets and rainbows and wild dreams.

"It's got a kitchen," Ms. Goolagong assured them. "Plus a sofa and chairs and bookshelves and whatever else. And two pondhouse pies sitting on the counter, dying to be eaten."

And off they went, Amy and Moo and Oliver the powerful lawyer and Ms. Goolagong, and Mom and Dad and Ms. Kopernikus, hiking toward the ditch and the bus and the road.

"It's nice to see you, Oliver," said Amy.

"It's nice to see you, too," Oliver replied. "It's been a while."

"A couple of hours," said Amy.

"Twenty-five years," said Oliver. "Quite enough time to think about everything you told us, long ago, in Elaine's cabin. Time enough to make quite a few plans."

Behind them, Ms. Goolagong was saying, "Yes, Ms. Wood, I have a medicine cabinet. You're welcome to check on your daughter's terrible, awful head wound. I hope we don't have to amputate. You're lucky it wasn't worse! They'll tell you all about it if you promise to remain calm. Why, these girls have been through more than you know in just a day. As for the rest of you—"

"I'm starved," said Oliver. "It was a long flight."

"Well, then," said the witch, "I believe I've got some

ham, and crackers, and perhaps a Tootsie Roll or two. If none of that appeals to you, there's a roasted third grader in the oven."

The parents jumped.

"Kidding," said the witch, leading the way across the ditch.

"Everyone knows you don't roast children," the girls heard her mutter to Oliver. "You have to boil them, or they scorch."

Amy and Moo winked at each other, sharing the same thought as they all trooped down the road toward Ms. Goolagong's house.

When we are old women, they said to each other, *we will sometimes behave quite strangely, and there's nothing anyone can do about it.*

Out of nowhere, seemingly, Tuba appeared from above in a storm of feathers and unsuitable words. He managed to land on Amy's outstretched arm, muttering, "They changed the Monopoly pieces. Why'd they want to go and do a thing like that?"

When I'm old, said Moo, *I'm going to wear costumes, not just clothes.*

Amy nodded. "I'm going to start with a new butterfly hoodie. I'll pay for it this time."

We could make one of those Chinese dragons, like they have in parades, with, like, forty people inside it. Except it

would be small enough for just two people, and whenever we
go into town, we'll go as a dragon.

Amy nodded thoughtfully.

"We could do a lot of crime experiments," she said, "disguised as a Chinese dragon."

She kept expecting Tuba to repeat something, but . . . nope. He was snoring.

"Of course," said Amy, "before all that, when I grow up, I'm going to be a witch."

Me too, said Moo.

"Me too," said Oliver.

"Me too!" laughed Ms. Goolagong.

"That's enough for me," snorted Tuba, talking in his sleep. "I need another chocolate chip cookie like I need another rear end."

ACKNOWLEDGMENTS

Hi.

Why are you reading the acknowledgments? The story is over. What exactly did you think you would find back here? A golden ticket? A secret code? A dead, mashed-up spider? (I found one of those in a book once. It was horrible, but also sort of fantastic.)

Anyhow, I'm *glad* you are reading the acknowledgments, because in this book, they are for YOU.

Yes, you, specifically.

Why?

Because you're the reader.

You're the whole reason this book—any book—even exists. If you weren't there to read it (if you didn't *choose* to read it), this book would . . . well, I think it would be very sad, for one thing. Don't you? It would be like a dancing bear named Charles putting on an outrageous, roaring ballet in the middle of the woods and dancing the BIG FINISH only to discover that everyone had gone home to watch TV instead. *Sniff*.

So I'm glad that you were there and that you read every word carefully and wisely—possibly with a sigh—all the way from beginning to end. You are this book's best friend.

Consider yourself acknowledged.

Now, there are other people who should be acknowledged. I mean, there are people who helped make the book happen. Like, helped me take out parts that were dumb and add things that were magical.

One of them is my agent, Michelle Brower. She has a dog named Jonathan. Sometimes she makes him wear costumes.

Another is my editor, Jenna Lettice. She likes to go hiking in places like Colorado. Her favorite character in this book is Tuba. She helped me see places in the book that needed to be less like dirty socks and more like chocolate and storms. I'm also grateful to senior editor Caroline Abbey, who was a big cheerleader for Amy, Moo, Ms. G., Oliver, and Tuba and helped bring them into the publishing world so that you could read about them. Thanks, Caroline!

There's my wife, Janine. She's a professor who writes books, and poems about snakes. And there's Jianna, my daughter. She's an excellent, *excellent* artist. I wrote this for her. I hope she likes it. If she doesn't, that's going to be awkward.

Thank you for reading the acknowledgments.

Maybe you should look at the next page, too. You never know what you'll find. Perhaps a possum . . . or a pizza . . .

ABOUT THE AUTHOR

Michael Poore has written several books and short stories for grown-ups. *Two Girls, a Clock, and a Crooked House* is his first novel for young people. He lives in Highland, Indiana, with his wife, the poet and activist Janine Harrison, and their daughter, Jianna.

 @michaelpoore227